ROBEк _ _ _ _

MW01526789

SOLITARY TREE

SOLITARY TREE is the exciting sequel to BLURRED LINE.
Will Mike be able to locate his abducted daughters? By reading
Solitary Tree you will be present, as Mike encounters the many
hurdles that are a part of everyday life.

ISBN 1542814677
EAN 978-1542814676

The cover for SOLITARY TREE was created by Robyn Prosser.
Robyn is an independent artist based in /Vernon BC. She uses a
wide variety of materials including Graphite, Acrylic, Oil, and
Water Color Paint. She has a large portfolio ranging from murals
to commissioned pieces which can be viewed at
www.RobynProsser.com.

Graphic design by Mark Prosser of Vernon, BC

SOLITARY TREE

PROLOUGE

Uttering a terse "See ya later Frank." Detective Mike Chance closed the vehicle door, and slowly wended his way towards the Airport terminal. Once inside the bustling Orange Grove regional airport, and had located the departures desk, he moved towards it to check-in for his flight home. Displaying his Gold Detective shield to confirm his identity, Mike surrendered his weapon for safe keeping during the flight. Not wanting to exchange meaningless, bothersome chatter with a fellow traveler for the next six hours, a thoroughly exhausted Mike requested a seat by himself.

Stowing his small carry-on bag in the overhead bin, Mike tiredly sank into the uncomfortable seat and closed his eyes. These past five days had been an emotional rollercoaster. Discovering that his missing daughters, four-year-old Desiree, and six-year-old Alicia were in fact alive, was the high point of the week. Realizing that he missed reuniting with them by a lousy three fucking days, had left him once again filled with anguish for his daughter's welfare, and a burning hatred for the people that committed this heinous crime against his children.

It was the discovery of a scrap of paper with the names of Mike's daughters; along with the name and address of the Jacobs by Constable Irene Ingalls of the South- bend Police department, that had led Mike to Orange Grove, Florida.

The Jacobs, who had harbored the girls these last eight months continued to thwart the local authorities. Their affluent, silver tongued lawyer claimed his clients were themselves the victims of a fraudulent adoption scheme. Mike and local detective Frank Hodgkin, had spent a mentally grueling week attempting to gain a confession from the Jacobs, but with their lawyer running interference for them, they continually plead ignorance to the

PROLOUGE

fact the girls they had adopted had been abducted. Even when faced with the fact their own servants had confirmed to the police, that money had changed hands for the girls they steadfastly maintained their innocence.

Despite their pleas of innocence, a case was slowly being built against them, due largely to the co-operation from their now mutinous servants.

Feeling a somewhat tentative poke to his shoulder, Mike opened his eyes to see a flight steward pointing at his waist miming the act of connecting the two ends of a seatbelt. Nodding his head in understanding, Mike located the seatbelt and with a metallic click joined the two ends together.

Arriving back at his cold, empty apartment the night before, Mike beat his shrilling alarm clock into submission. Rising from what felt like yet another sleepless night, in a never-ending parade of sleepless nights, he made his way to the bathroom, hoping that cold water would ease the burning behind his eyelids. Gazing into the bathroom mirror, Mike barely recognized the face staring back at him. With bloodshot eyes that felt scratched by windblown sand, the anguish that he has been living with these past eight months was clearly evidenced in the deep furrows tracking across his forehead. At only thirty-two years old, Mike can readily see random dashes of gray hair appearing in his curly black hair. Splashing cold water on his face he blindly reached for the towel that was always hanging beside the sink, not feeling it he opened his eyes and spotted it lying discarded in the corner of the bathroom. Closing his eyes, he braced his arms on the edge of the sink, bending his head allowed the water to slowly wend its way down his face, joined by a lone, salty, tear.

Walking through the three-bedroom apartment with merely a towel wrapped about his mid-section, Mike could swear he heard the ghostly laughter of his girls as he chased them, or crying as they suffered through the pain of teething. Stopping in the kitchen, he was positive he could detect the tantalizing aroma of hot, spicy Mexican food that his wife Adele loved to prepare for

PROLOUGE

him. Not sure what his estranged wife Adele's response will be, Mike knew that he must call her and advise her of the what he had discovered in Orange Grove.

Wondering if the mobility number that he had for Adele was still current he decided to try it anyways.

After the third ring a voice that he remembered so well answered. "What do you want Mike? Did you already receive the documents?"

"Hi Adele, its Mike. What documents?" queried Mike wondering what the hell she was talking about.

"Never mind Mike, I repeat what do you want?" asked Adele in an acid laden voice.

"Adele, I have discovered that our girls were not taken randomly. It seems that Ellen the girl's caregiver is sergeant O'Mallory's niece and they conspired together to take our children. They sold them to a couple in Orange Grove Florida. This couple had them for almost eight months, I only missed the girls by three lousy days." Following this abbreviated revelation, the last thing Mike expected was the continued silence from Adele. "Adele, are you there? "Did you hear what I said?" asked a dumbfounded Mike.

"Of course, I did! So, what are you looking for Mike? Are you looking for me to exonerate you for the loss of our children?"

Completely taken aback by Adele's cryptic response and the loathing in her voice, Mike responded with unrestrained anger of his own. Telling Adele that he had lived these last months overwhelmed with guilt, the only thing saving him from suicide was the thought of one-day reuniting with his daughters. With anger clipping his words, he went on to explain that Alicia and Desiree were not taken because he was overdue by thirty minutes, but likely taken thirty minutes after Adele dropped them off.

Interrupting Mike with a loud snort of derision, Adele impatiently asked Mike what he was seeking.

PROLOUGE

"Seeking? What do you think I'm seeking!", thundered an incredulous Mike. "I'm seeking our daughters and the people responsible for abducting them."

"Sounds to me like you're looking for an excuse to blame me.

That I failed the girls by not properly investigating Ellen, I remember when I asked you what you thought about Ellen, you merely grunted and left it up to me. Think about this Mike, if as you say Ellen is your old sergeant's niece, what did you do to piss him off to the point they would take our children? Mike! I have moved on, in fact I thought maybe you were calling about a completely different matter. We will never again be the perfect family you so desperately craved."

"So, you're saying that you have given up hope of ever finding our girls. How could you possibly say this Adele!" cried an unbelieving Mike. "These are our children, our flesh and blood!"

"Like I said Mike, the reality is, they are gone. Yes, I loved them, yes, they will always have a place in my heart, but they are gone. I have moved on; I will not be one of those people you see on the news who spend their entire lives searching for something that no longer exists."

Not wanting to believe what his estranged wife was telling him, Mike responded with resignation and defeat reducing his voice to a barely audible whisper, informing Adele that he will never stop searching for his daughters.

Pushing the end call button on his phone, Mike hurried to his bedroom and dressing quickly, vacated the home that has now transformed into a tomb.

CHAPTER ONE

At seven-thirty on a cold, wet, blustery morning, Detective Mike Chance pushed his way through the revolving doors and entered his precinct. Stopping for a minute to brush a few errant raindrops from his jacket, he almost smiled as he absorbed the bedlam of the first floor, realizing that somethings never change.

A look of pure hatred crossed his countenance as he gazed upon the Sergeants desk that was until recently, occupied by Gwyn O'Mallory. Mike discovered during his brief sojourn to Orange Grove, Florida that O'Mallory had been the driving force behind his daughter's abduction.

Striding across the large, open room to the stairwell, Mike ascended the steps to the Detective's Division on the second floor. Entering the much quieter room Mike was surprised at the reception he received. The dozen or so Detectives already in the room, warmly welcomed him back with smiles and waves, some even approached him to shake his hand. Mike appreciated the fact that they were being politely circumspect, avoiding any questions concerning his daughter's whereabouts.

Arriving at his desk and seating himself, he found it somewhat ironic that the Delveccio file was the first one he spied, this was the very first file he had encountered, when he was made a Detective. Mike's resolve to capture or kill the brothers had been significantly reinforced upon learning they had played a major role in the abduction of his daughter's.

SOLITARY TREE

Feeling somewhat at loose ends, he began to draw concentric circles on his legal pad, the emerging pattern of circles with names, appeared to have O'Mallory as the focal point.

Mike's deliberations were interrupted when he heard a commotion at the doorway entering the squad room. Looking up he was amazed to see the precinct Captain, Stephen Chamberlain and his entourage heading towards the vacant lieutenant's office

The stately looking captain with the warm smile, was highly respected within the precinct, having worked his way up through the ranks, from a rookie patrol cop to his present office, he had managed to instill in others his penchant for honesty and bravery. It had been said by many, that behind the fatherly smile and warm blue eyes, was a vat of molten steel, known to erupt at the slightest threat to his beloved police department.

Bringing up the rear of this noteworthy group was the notorious Lieutenant William Bowers, well known throughout the precinct to be the Captains personal hatchet man. With his angular shaped head swiveling on a pair of emaciated shoulders, he glanced around the room, much like Raptor would in search of prey. With his curiosity now aroused, Mike leaned back in his chair and watched with interest as they filed into the vacant office and closed the door.

The door had barely closed when it re-opened with Bowers making a beeline towards Mike's desk. Mike calmly watched him approach with a feigned combination of dis-interest and trepidation.

Stopping directly in front of Mike, and jerking his thumb over his shoulder in the direction he just came from, he advised Mike his presence was required in the office. Not wanting to give Bowers the satisfaction of knowing how nervous he felt with this declaration, Mike continued to stare up at him for thirty seconds before slowly rising from his chair.

Making his way around the desk, Mike gave Bowers a subtle bump with his shoulder, subtle enough to not be construed as striking a senior officer, but at the same time sending a clear message.

SOLITARY TREE

Resigning himself to what appeared to be the inevitable, Mike entered the room fully prepared to be dismissed. Deciding to fire the first salvo, Mike stated with a clearly sardonic twist to his words. "There's enough brass in here to start a band."

This statement was met with stony silence until the stately looking Captain began to chuckle, there-by allowing the others to cautiously join in.

"You're absolutely right Mike," returned the captain seated behind the lone desk. "But I fear they would make a piss poor band," replying with a huge smile. Returning once more to a serious demeanor, staring hard at Mike, the Captain continued. "I have a strong hunch you think you were about to be dismissed, if that were the case I would have simply sent Bowers. In fact, Mike, I'm hoping that quite the opposite happens here. The Police Department needs to be shaken up, recently there have been too many family and friends in the wrong positions. We need to adopt a new direction, and hopefully you will represent that new direction."

Wholly surprised as well as intrigued at what was being said, Mike was relieved knowing that he is not about to be fired.

"While you were on detached duty in Orange Grove, your predecessor Bill Watson had been re-assigned, this means I need a new Chief of Detectives." Pointing towards an unopened file resting on the desk in front of him, he explained that it was a mental fitness report from the Police Department's counselor Jackie Nelson. In it she stated that despite intense personal trauma, you retain the ability to function at a level that far exceeds your peers. "These are the traits that I am looking for Mike," declared the Captain. "People like yourself that will allow the Department to once again be respected, not ridiculed by the public. So, what do you say?"

Caught completely flatfooted by this turn of events Mike looked down and studied his feet for a moment while he collected his thoughts. Raising his head, he scrutinized the Captain and with a small smile began speaking.

SOLITARY TREE

"You were right Captain, at first I had thought I was about to be dismissed. I am honored that you feel I possess the qualities you are searching for. I won't insult your intelligence by stating there might be others better qualified for this position, as I'm sure you have spent a significant amount of time deciding who might be best. I humbly accept this new challenge you have offered, but I would also like to request a few personal days to tidy up some loose ends."

Rising quickly from his chair the Captain reached across the desk and shook Mike's hand and congratulated him, he told Mike to take a week off and when he returned this office would be his.

Then as quickly as they blown in, the Captain and his minions took their leave, everyone except Bowers, shaking Mike's hand and offering their support.

Standing in the wake of the departing brass, Mike was snapped back to reality when he heard his name called.

CHAPTER TWO

"Hey Mike, let me be the first to offer congratulations," declared Detective Mario Vessotti at the same time reaching for Mike's hand and shaking it vigorously.

"Thanks Mario. Did you guys know about this?"

"You know the department Mike. There's no way anything is kept secret for more than an hour."

"True enough," remarked Mike with a wry smile.

"Anyway, I just wanted to let you know that a couple of dead guys have been discovered in one of those deserted warehouses on Fremont."

Staring at Mario, Mike quipped. "Guess that means I'm back in the city."

Even though he was not officially back on duty, Mike decided to hop in his car and drive to the location of the deceased. Parking his car amidst the array of both marked and unmarked police vehicles, Mike headed towards an open door. Seeing the Medical Examiners van, he idly wondered if the gum chewing Mel Webster had caught this case. Still twenty feet away from the open doorway the cloying stench of decomposing bodies caused Mike to gag.

SOLITARY TREE

Coming to a halt beside Mike, a uniformed patrolman handed a mask to him commenting, "Here take this, it helps a bit." "Thanks," murmured a grateful Mike. Donning the proffered mask Mike once again headed towards the open doorway.

Once inside the inky darkness of the cavernous building, Mike observed a flurry of activity at the base of a staircase.

Approaching the area artificially lit up with portable halogen lights, the stench of decomposing flesh was clearly detectable even through the mask.

Deciding that since he was not here in any official capacity, he remained in the shadows of the bright lights and studied the scene laid out before him. It was clear given the chaotic way the two bodies are intertwined they must have tumbled down the long staircase. It was only when he moved slightly to one side that he could discern the faces of the deceased, and was shocked to realize that he was viewing the notorious Delveccio brothers.

Mike felt absolutely no remorse with the demise of the Delveccio brothers, the world will be a better place with them dead. With the aid of their Uncle Gwynn, the former desk sergeant at the precinct, they had managed to evade prosecution for their many crimes. Suddenly the arrest of Mike's ex-partner, and now fugitive from justice Larry Donovan replayed itself in Mike's mind. When Mike had informed Larry that the Delveccio's liked to talk, Larry had laughed and sharply retorted. "Their pretty close mouthed these days."

Based on what he knew; Mike can only assume that Larry had played a significant role in the brother's deaths. Watching with an air of detachment for a few minutes as the crime scene techs went about their business, Mike pondered his own immediate plans.

Abruptly turning on his heel, Mike's long ground eating strides soon propelled him back outside leaving behind the reek of death, removing the mask and gulping fresh air, Mike walked back to his vehicle.

SOLITARY TREE

Once inside his car he began driving with no clear destination in mind, until he happened across a playground. Allowing the car to come to a slow halt against the curb, the ghost of a smile appeared at the corner of his mouth as he watched numerous children on swing sets and slides. With the morning's rain, having given way to blue skies and warm sun, the park was alive with exuberant youngsters.

Opening the door to his car, he was met with the sound of laughter emanating from the children's throats as they played. Walking towards an adult sized swing set Mike stopped, bent over and untying his shoes removed them and his socks. The feel of soft grass beneath his feet, as he curled his toes was exquisite, he couldn't remember the last time that he had allowed himself this simple pleasure. The fresh, clean, slightly acerbic aroma of the still damp grass flushed the last vestiges of death from Mike's nostrils.

Glancing at the construction of the swing he had serious doubts about its ability to support his weight, deciding the nearby picnic table looked infinitely safer walked the short distance to it and sat down. Retrieving his phone from a shirt pocket, lost in thought Mike gently tapped it against the table top, arriving at a decision he punched in a number and waited for the call to connect.

Lamenting the fact that he felt a sense of relief hearing the call go to Irene's voice mail, he began to leave his message. Telling her machine, he would not be able to return to South bend to see her as there are too loose ends that needed to be addressed. Hearing a click Mike thought he may have reached the end of her recording time until he heard Irene's voice.

"Hey Michael, sorry I was in a meeting. I just slipped out for a minute. So, what were you saying?"

Reiterating what he had said Mike realized that he need not have worried. Irene advised him she was now the acting Chief of Police in South bend and felt that she needed to focus her energies to that end. So, with both Mike and Irene, promising to stay in touch, the call came to a quick and merciful end.

With his daughters gone, his wife deserting him and now Irene lost to him, Mike felt completely abandoned. Reminiscent of that fateful day when everything changed. Eighteen years old, just two weeks before his high school graduation, two cops showed up at his parents' home, and bluntly informed Mike his parents had been killed by a drunk driver while they were crossing the road.

They had walked to the corner store to get an ice cream cone, and it cost them their lives. It was at that point Mike understood the term alone, there was no one left in the world that cared if he died or lived. At eighteen years of age, he was solely responsible for arranging his parent's funeral, there was only one person that Mike thought he should contact, that was his father's brother Ki. His father had explicitly warned Mike about Ki and what he represented, so it was with some reluctance that Mike contacted his uncle and informed him of his parent's death, he was rewarded with a mere grunt, accompanied by the sound of the call being ended. Meandering through the empty house, Mike walked up to the chess board that he and his father had enjoyed matching wits against each other in the game of war placed on the small table in the Livingroom's alcove. Studying the placement of the remaining chess pieces in the match that will never see a winner, Mike reached across the chess board and flipped the game clock onto its face, no longer will time be a factor in this match.

The funeral service was attended solely by Mike, and the funeral home director, after three minutes of listening to the director stumble through a speech about people he never knew, Mike got up in disgust and retrieving the urns that contained his parents remains left.

The next day, when Mike answered a knock on the door of the ground floor apartment, he was not at all surprised to see it was the seriously overweight, belligerent apartment building manager Clive.

SOLITARY TREE

The building manager brusquely informed Mike that if he planned on continuing to live in the apartment, the rent would be due in two days.

"How much is the rent?" asked Mike.

"Fifteen Hundred," grunted Clive.

"I don't have that much money," protested Mike.

"Not my problem, if you don't have the rent then you need to be out in two days," declared an uncaring Clive.

Mike failed to attend his high school graduation ceremony, the few friends he had pleaded with him to attend, but without his parent's there to witness the event it would have been a hollow victory.

The next eighteen months saw Mike drift from one meaningless job to another, much like a rudderless boat, powerless to control its own destiny.

On a sunny Wednesday morning, on his way to another meaningless job, Mike witnessed an unkempt, disreputable looking man who appeared to be about forty years old, knock an elderly lady to the ground and snatch her purse. Witnessing this event Mike quickly intervened, and with the past eighteen months of bottled up rage at his parent's senseless death motivating him, the unfortunate recipient of his fury was soon lying unconscious on the sidewalk with blood streaming from his nose. It was at that point that Mike decided that he wanted to be a cop, and perhaps help put an end to the carnage created by people who put themselves above the law.

Swiveling on the hard-wooden surface of the table's attached bench, stretching his legs out then leaning backwards against the table's rounded edge, Mike watched with a soul shattering sense of loss, as some of the children were playing tag, and others shrieking with feigned terror as they plummeted down the miniature slide.

SOLITARY TREE

Turning back to face the table, Mike extracted his notebook from his shirt pocket and with grim determination began to write. He's sick and tired of being pushed around by life, it's time he pushed back, and pushed back fucking hard. He's weary of the death and destroyed lives that are part of his daily existence, he never envisioned his chosen career being this difficult. As a rookie cop, Mike had railed against the pervasive cynicism with embittered veteran cops regarding people in general, challenging those veteran cops to believe that for the most part people will do the right thing. Regretfully, Mike has come to the realization that people will only do the right thing when it best serves their interests. Mike, no longer harbors false illusions regarding the basic good in people, it has been proven time and again to him that not only is it naïve, it could also prove to be deadly. Prioritizing what needed to be done he examined his list, changing a couple of items, nodded his head in satisfaction at this newly found direction. The one item that he has no control over is his ex- partner Larry Donovan, the mere thought of his hated ex-partner transformed Mike's cheeks to a prickly crimson with the sudden influx of hot blood, Mike has sworn to shoot him on sight but, unfortunately Larry appears to have vanished.

Sensing the rapid approach of someone behind him, Mike turned his head and watched with amusement as a young boy with bright blue hair chased his errant soccer ball. Capturing the ball, the youngster noticed Mike watching him.

Smiling in amusement at the bright blue hair, Mike asked him how he came to have hair that color.

Staring back at Mike with curiosity, tinged with fear, he informed Mike in his young boy's high pitched voice that his sister did it. Continuing to stare at Mike the young boy asked him. "Why are you sitting here Mister?"

SOLITARY TREE

Noticing Mike's shoes and socks on the picnic table he
informed Mike in no uncertain terms, that he should have his
shoes on as his mother had warned him there are used needles
from addicts hiding in the grass.

"Why thank-you for the warning young man, what is your
name? asked Mike.

"My name is Benjamin Pierce," stated the blue haired boy
proudly.

"Well Benjamin Pierce, it's been really enjoyable talking to
you."

"Hey Mister, why aren't you at work? Are you lost or
something?" queried the inquisitive Benjamin.

"Not anymore Benjamin!" announced Mike emphatically. Then
following the wise Benjamin's advice, Mike stooped over and
put his socks and shoes back on. Mike was about to say good-
bye to young Benjamin when he realized the lad was already
safely back amongst his friends, pointing his finger back in
Mikes direction.

CHAPTER THREE

   Walking with a renewed sense of purpose and confidence, Mike spied a lonely relic from a past generation. Altering his course slightly he arrived at the much-abused phone booth. He was not surprised to see the phone's handset lying discarded in a corner of the small enclosure, long ago severed from its base. Phone booths dotted about the city had until the last few years been a sanctuary that people could enter, close the door and briefly escape the chaos of life while connecting with others. Unfortunately, this was no longer the case, the few remaining phone booths are like this one, just a broken reminder of what used to be. Spotting the object of his hunt dangling from a frayed length of cable, wishing he had a pair of gloves Mike hesitantly and with some trepidation lifted the bulky form of the phone directory and placed it on the miniscule shelf. Leafing through the heavily stained, musky smelling book, Mike found the page he was searching for and feeling a minor pang of guilt separated the page from its spine.

   Sitting in his car, perusing the directory page he placed a call to one of the listed offices. Surprised that he could get an appointment right away, Mike started his vehicle and headed towards his new beginning.

   Entering the Law offices of Lynch and Associates, Mike moved toward the receptionist's desk. Introducing himself, he was told by the young bottle blonde seated behind the counter, completely immersed in filing her finger nails to take a seat and someone will see him shortly. Shaking his head in amusement, Mike walked the few steps to what he assumed to be the waiting area, taking a seat began to think that he may have picked the wrong lawyer.

SOLITARY TREE

Mike had no sooner sat down, when he heard the receptionist advise an unseen party that his eleven o'clock appointment was here.

"Well for Pete's sake Angela, I'm paying you to be my receptionist, not manicure your nails, so would you please show him to my office!" barked the unseen male voice.

Listening to this brief reprimand, Mike once again thought he should re-visit his choice of legal representation. Hearing the click of high heeled shoes on the mahogany colored, faux hardwood floor, Mike was already standing when Angela appeared around the corner.

"He will see you now, please follow me," muttered the chastised Angela. Proceeding down a short hallway she walked through an open door. With a quizzical glance at Mike she asked him. "Did you say your name was Mike?"

Nodding his head in the affirmative, she introduced him to John Lynch, the grey haired, bespectacled individual, seated behind an oversized desk strewn with papers.

Rising from his high-backed chair to shake Mike's hand John apologized, explaining that Angela is his niece and is regretfully, not highly motivated.

"So, Mike what brings you to my office today?" Nodding his head in the direction of Mike's gold detective shield he continued with a warm smile. "Since you haven't produced a warrant for my arrest I assume you're here on personal business."

Mincing no words, Mike informed John that he would like to get a divorce.

"Okay we can do that. But before we begin Mike, do you happen to have a dollar bill on you?"

Unable to fit his large hand into his pants pocket while seated Mike rose from his chair and retrieved a rumpled dollar bill. Once again seated, he passed the bill to John with a perplexed look.

"Thank-you Mike. Now, attorney client privilege is in place, I am bound by law not to divulge any details of our conversation."

SOLITARY TREE

Reaching for his yellow colored legal pad, John began to scribble some notes, finished he looked up at Mike and asked. "Okay Mike, who would you like to petition for divorce?"

"My wife," bluntly declared Mike, wondering to himself who else he could possibly want a divorce from.

"I'm sorry, of course it's would be your wife. I was asking for her name," apologized John.

"Oh." exclaimed Mike with a sheepish smile, then provided John with the required information.

"Okay Mike, are there children involved?"

Albeit reluctantly, Mike advised John of the situation with his missing daughters. Leaning backwards in his high-backed leather chair, he listened carefully as Mike elucidated the situation with his daughters.

John was immediately struck by the depth of misery evident in Mike's voice and body language as he talked.

Scribbling a few quick notes John studied what he had written then calmly began speaking. "This is a most unusual situation Mike; my suggestion would be to petition for divorce on the grounds of irreconcilable differences. The fact that you have had virtually no contact with Adele for nine months now will sway the judge. The matter of who will receive custody of your missing daughters will in my humble opinion, be postponed until they are located."

With the anger and resentment, he felt towards Adele clear in his voice, Mike urged John to proceed with the divorce.

"Very well Mike. I will have these papers drawn up and ready for your signature by weeks' end."

Rising from his chair Mike thanked him, and with John escorting him out of the office, Mike felt like a burden had been lifted from his shoulders.

SOLITARY TREE

Knowing the lightness in his step was linked directly to this irrevocable path he had chosen, and enjoying the feeling immensely, Mike decided to walk the three blocks to his next appointment.

Having only covered a short distance, Mike felt the short hairs on the back of his neck alert him to the fact he was being watched. Stopping and feigning interest in a furniture store's wares, Mike studied the street through the reflection in the glass window. Searching in vain for whatever it was that triggered his alarm system, laughing out loud at what he discovered, he turned around and gazed at an oversized eye painted on the fascia of a smaller store.

Staring at the eye Mike was certain that the painted black pupil moved. To the immediate left of the mysterious eye was a large red banner declaring, "Gwendolyn Sees all."

Intrigued by the sign and what it might represent, Mike acting on a whim decided to find out. Entering the poorly lit store that exuded an odor vaguely reminiscent of mothballs, Mike made his way towards the counter. Looking over the counter, he observed a young man so captivated by the book he was reading he was completely unaware of Mike's presence. Knocking softly on the counter to gain the reader's attention Mike was unprepared for the reaction he received.

"Holy Shit! Where did you come from?" exclaimed the startled reader.

"Outside," responded Mike, smiling humorously at the reader.

Regaining his equilibrium, the young man smiled back at Mike and explained that he was the first person to walk into the store in a week.

"Who is Gwendolyn? And what does she see?" queried Mike.

Still smiling, the young man proudly informed Mike that Gwendolyn was his sister, and she possesses the capacity to read peoples fortunes.

Looking askance at the earnest young man, Mike decided to take his leave.

SOLITARY TREE

Unwilling to see the one customer he has had in a week leave, the young man hopped off his chair and entered the same area Mike was in through a side door.

"Hey Mister, wait a minute please," implored the young man.

Turning back to explain that he does not have time for such idiocy, Mike was flabbergasted when he noticed the young man of perhaps twenty years old, was only about four feet tall. Walking back to the counter and re-examining the chair that had until recently been occupied by the short person, Mike discerned the presence of several pillows.

Looking up at Mike, the young man shrugged his shoulders in resignation and explained that he had dwarfism.

"By the way my name is Geraldo. Now, I would like to take you in the back to see my sister. She really can read people's fortunes," insisted Geraldo.

Deciding that he had nothing to lose, Mike agreed to see his sister.

"Hey that's great!" chirped an exultant Geraldo. "That will be forty dollars please."

Grimacing at the news that this moment of idiocy was now going to cost him forty bucks, Mike reluctantly removed a pair of twenties from his wallet.

Grasping the money in a hand that was inordinately large for someone so small, Geraldo beckoned for Mike to follow him. Entering an even smaller room that was equally musty smelling as the one they had just vacated, Mike was amazed when he met Gwendolyn, who was equal in height to Mike at six feet three inches. With her long, fiery red hair, eyes the color of polished jade, and almost translucent skin she certainly didn't fit Mike's pre-conceived image of a fortune teller.

Observing Mike's surprise at how tall his sister was, Geraldo chirped "She doesn't even like basketball."

"Go on, leaves us munchkin," bantered Gwendolyn with a mixture of love and tolerance in her voice, as she watched her miniscule brother leave the room.

SOLITARY TREE

Regaining her seat at the lone, battered table, she gestured for Mike to sit on one of the equally battered chairs.

Feeling uncomfortable as Gwendolyn stared at him, Mike was ready to leave the room when Gwendolyn gently asked him who he had lost.

"What makes you think I have lost someone?" enquired Mike with a sharp edge in his voice.

"It is written clearly on your face. You have recently lost someone very dear to you."

"Where's your crystal ball?" questioned a cynical Mike buying himself time to decide if he wanted to impart his story to this lady.

Smiling at Mike's question she informed him that when her mother used to tell people's fortunes, one of her clients grew upset and broke it.

"Really? Imagine that," replied Mike not bothering to mask his cynicism.

Gently laughing at Mike's obvious dis-belief, she informed him that she had no idea what a crystal ball even looked like.

"What I do know, is that looking at you I detect great distress and loss. Do you happen to have a picture of the person lost to you?"

Reaching into his left shirt pocket, Mike extracted a picture of Desiree and Alicia his two missing daughters, and passed it to Gwendolyn.

"I notice you carry the picture closest to your heart. What beautiful children, what are their names?" enquired Gwendolyn softly.

Almost mesmerized by Gwendolyn's soft, slightly accented voice, Mike relayed the girl's names to her. Watching closely as Gwendolyn closed her eyes, several minutes' slip by with no response. Mike was ready to ask for his picture back, when he noticed minute beads of sweat appear on her forehead. Looking at the picture clutched in Gwendolyn's hand, Mike watched in astonishment as the picture appeared to vibrate.

SOLITARY TREE

Hearing a low moan escape from Gwendolyn, Mike was spellbound by what was happening to her.

Breathing rapidly, with the tiny beads of perspiration now fast becoming rivulets on her brow, a loud moan issued from her throat followed closely by. "The girls are alive. I see a large body of water, there is a solitary tree bearing a single leaf," and with that her eyes snap wide open and gasping for air her head slumped forward onto the table.

Instantly alarmed for Gwendolyn's wellbeing, Mike leapt from his chair, opening the door leading into the main room of the office, urgently summoned Geraldo.

As Geraldo, calmly reassured Mike that she will be fine, he explained that what happens to his sister, is like an epileptic seizure, she just requires a couple of minutes to relax. No sooner had Geraldo finished his explanation, Gwendolyn lifted her head, and with a weak smile directed at Mike, asked him if she had helped.

"You don't remember what you said?" asked a still concerned Mike.

"I never do," she replied looking completely drained. Handing the picture back to Mike she remarked tiredly "If you don't mind I need to go lie down now."

Accepting the sweat soaked picture and with a final concerned look for Gwendolyn, Mike thanked them both and quickly exited the room.

Once more on the sidewalk, with the warm sun shining on his face and enjoying the taste of the fresh air, Mike wondered at what had occurred. Knowing that he had been in the store for less than thirty minutes, Mike was unable to shake the feeling that he had lost several hours. Being told his girls are alive, a large body of water, a solitary tree bearing a single leaf, had created more questions than answers. Wanting to believe with his whole being that what Gwendolyn had imparted was true, a part of Mike couldn't help but think he had been the target of a cruel hoax.

SOLITARY TREE

Enjoying the sun on his face, Mike walked the short distance to his now much delayed appointment, accepting the fact that although statistics have proven the odds against locating his daughters were undeniably against him, he would exhaust every means at his disposal before he ever gave up his search, knowing in his heart that the day he admitted they wouldn't be found would be his last day on earth.

"Gun! Gun! She has a gun!" screamed a terrified young girl as she hurtled past Mike.

Suddenly Mike became aware of many people shouting the word gun. Stopping an older lady Mike asked what was going on, and was told that there's a crazy lady in the intersection pointing a gun at everyone. Dashing the thirty yards to the intersection, Mike confirmed what he had been told. Standing in the middle of the intersection, brandishing a gun was a female that Mike guessed to be about twenty years old.

Unobtrusively drawing his firearm from its holster, and holding it out of sight beside his leg, Mike began to crabwalk towards the young lady.

Hoping to de-escalate the situation, Mike called out to her advising her that he's Detective Mike Chance with the Metro-City Department, he then asked her what her name was.

Ignoring Mike, she continued to scream obscenities at everyone and no one, while randomly pointing her weapon. With only fifteen feet now separating them, Mike once again introduced himself and asked her what her name was. Becoming aware of Mike's proximity, she focused her attention entirely on him.

"No!" screamed the distraught young lady. "You want to pretend that you can help me, but you can't. No one can!" she howled in obvious distress.

Under the assumption, she had ingested some sort of illicit drug, and was experiencing a very bad reaction, Mike endeavored to pour oil on these obviously troubled waters when he enquired if she had taken any drugs recently.

SOLITARY TREE

"I don't do drugs," she shrieked. "When I take the meds, the doctor gave me I can't see them."

"Who is it you can't see?" asked Mike evenly.

"The demons. There're everywhere," she cried. "They want to hurt me," she sobbed.

"Do you see them now?" Mike asked as realization dawned on him that this young lady suffered from something that was far beyond his ken.

Struggling to think of something that may help to defuse the situation, Mike again asked her what her name was.

Appearing not to have heard Mike's question, she once again began to wave the gun around indiscriminately.

Watching her eyes closely from the fifteen feet that separated them, Mike vainly searched for any clue as to what he might say that would calm her down to the point where this might end peacefully. Thinking about these demons she had mentioned, Mike asked her where there at.

"There're right behind you," she informed Mike, her fear filled eyes locked on something over Mike's shoulder.

"Tell you what," suggested a desperate Mike. "If you place your gun on the ground, I will arrest these fuckin demons for harassing you."

"No good," she sobbed brokenly. "They can't be arrested," tapping the side of her head with the barrel of the gun she quietly explained to Mike they are in her head.

Having said that she began to slowly and inexorably raise the heavy weapon and point it in Mike's direction.

"Do not raise that weapon!" commanded Mike. "I repeat do not raise that weapon!"

Choosing to ignore his commands, she continued to raise the gun. Knowing that he had been left no recourse Mike was forced to raise his own weapon, and repeat his command for her to drop the gun. Using two hands she had nearly raised the heavy weapon to point directly at Mike, who now franticly implored her to put the gun down, or he will be forced to shoot.

SOLITARY TREE

Ignoring Mike's pleas, she calmly advised him that her name was Jennifer. Staring at Mike she lip-synced the word "Sorry" and brought the gun the rest of the way up to point directly at Mike.

Having no choice left but to protect himself, Mike fired two rounds into the female's upper torso. The sudden, and catastrophic impact from the two missiles caused her to fall backwards into a lifeless heap. With the explosive sound of his firearm still ringing in his ears, Mike slowly approached the female, kicking the gun away from her body, bent down to check for signs of life.

Not finding a pulse, Mike felt his adrenalin fired body begin to relax, as once again sounds re- entered his consciousness.

"Hey Detective is she dead?" asked an approaching patrolman. Gazing up at the blue uniform Mike confirmed that she was deceased, and ordered the patrolman to secure the discarded weapon.

Following Mike's orders, he picked up the weapon and removed the clip, then working the slide to eject any round located in the chamber.

"Uh, Detective, this gun is empty."

"What do you mean it's empty?" barked Mike.

"I mean there are no bullets in this gun," returned the patrolman.

Standing up Mike covered the few steps to where the uniformed cop was holding the weapon for Mike's inspection.

Verifying the fact that the gun was indeed empty. "What the fuck?" murmured Mike, completely baffled by the empty gun.

Staring at Mike the young patrolman quietly asked him if he would like a bullet to be placed in the gun.

Realizing full well what the patrolman was offering, and its ramifications, Mike stared back and in a voice, that brooked no argument, informed the young cop that tampering with evidence was an indictable offence.

"I was hoping you would say that," stated the cop.

SOLITARY TREE

Walking back to the body of the deceased female, a troubled Mike stared down at her, wondering what could have gone so horribly wrong in her short life, that compelled her to take this action.

Completely engrossed with his thoughts, Mike was surprised when he realized the scene was now crawling with cops.

Knowing full well that he had been left with no recourse other than the use of deadly force, did nothing to ease the abject sorrow he felt at this tragic loss of life.

Watching as a somewhat older, swarthy skinned plain clothes cop approached, and introduced himself as Detective Herman Diaz from the twelfth precinct, Mike introduced himself and related that he was also a detective at the twelfth precinct.

"My car is two blocks over I will go get it, and meet you at the precinct," stated Mike.

"Given the circumstances I would prefer it if you gave me your keys and I will have someone take it to the precinct for you," stated Diaz.

"What the fuck?" exclaimed Mike slightly annoyed at the older Detective. "I can't drive my own car now!"

"Come on Chance, you know the fuckin drill, I can't let you leave the scene of a shooting unescorted."

Snorting in disgust Mike was about to argue further when a now impatient Diaz growled, "Why you busting my balls here Chance? You got something to hide?".

"Fuck you Diaz!" blazed Mike, as hot blood transformed his cheeks from their normal toffee color to a flaming red hue.

Holding out his hand Diaz then ordered Mike to surrender his weapon. Knowing that Diaz was just following procedure did nothing to take the sting out of having to relinquish his weapon.

CHAPTER FOUR

"You about done here now?" queried an impatient Mike.

"Ya that should just about cover it," commented Diaz reviewing Mike's written statement. With a slight smirk, Diaz added that Internal Affairs may want to have a chat with Mike.

Hearing a knock on the door of the interview room, both Diaz and Mike looked up as Detective Hans Albright opened the door and leaned into the room.

"Hey Mike. How you doing? Just wanted to let you know everyone out here has your back. Oh yea, and congratulations on your appointment as Chief of Detectives," nodding his head in the direction of Diaz, Albright retreated and closed the door.

Staring at Mike in what has now become a very pregnant silence, Diaz growled. "You're going to be my boss?"

Returning the stare, Mike confirmed that starting next week he will be the new Chief of Detectives.

"Are we done here?" demanded Mike.

As though gauging his new boss, Diaz continued to glare at Mike for the space of a few heartbeats, before mentioning that Mike could retrieve his weapon from downstairs. Stopping at the closed door of the interview room, Mike turned back to face Diaz, asking him if he always went by the book.

Staring up at Mike from his seated position, Diaz responded dryly. "If we don't go by the book, then what's the point of having a book."

Nodding his head in agreement at these sage words, Mike exited the stale air of the interview room, deciding that his weapon could wait downstairs, he headed in the direction of his new office.

SOLITARY TREE

Inside the sanctuary of his office, he closed and locked the door, moving to the windows that looked out upon the large room that was home to the Twelfth Precincts Twenty Detective's, he closed the dirty, yellow stained venetian blinds. With his cave now secured against trespassers, Mike sank into the high-backed leather chair.

Leaning his elbows on the desk, and cradling his forehead with intertwined fingers, Mike closed his eyes and allowed his mind to escape into a thoughtless void. Hearing the doorknob to his office rattle as though someone was attempting to enter, Mike reluctantly forced his mind to return from the peaceful void it had temporarily escaped to.

Un-locking the door Mike came face to face with a concerned looking Albright.

"Hey, you alright Mike?"

"Ya fine," growled Mike.

"The guys said you locked the door and closed the blinds. Was getting a little concerned given today's events."

"I appreciate your concern, and yes I'm fine," stated Mike.

"Okay just checking," and with that Albright backed out of the office, purposely leaving the door open.

Knowing that he had three more days before officially back on duty, Mike decided to head downstairs to retrieve his weapon. Exiting the precinct building, Mike immediately noticed a young, scholarly looking individual with a colorful bouquet of flowers clutched in his left hand. Pushing himself off the side of the building that he had been leaning against, he headed in Mike's direction.

Approaching Mike, the individual politely asked if he was Detective Michael Chance. Affirming that he was indeed Michael Chance, he was surprised when the individual produced a brown manila type envelope placed it into Mike's hand, and pronounced. "Michael Chance. You've been served!"

Astonished at this development, Mike shouted at the rapidly disappearing server. "Hey! What about the flowers?"

SOLITARY TREE

Turning back to face Mike with a highly contagious smile, he informed Mike that although he was sure Mike was a nice guy, the flowers were for his girlfriend.

Opening the legal sized envelope, and withdrawing the enclosed document, the words Divorce Decree leapt off the page at him.

Escaping the main current of pedestrians, Mike retired to the quiet back eddy recently occupied by the server to peruse the document. After reading the brief document, Mike now knew what Adele had been referring to. Projecting a look that hovered somewhere between mirth and dejection, Mike murmured to himself. "Guess this means she doesn't love you anymore."

Extracting his wallet, he dug out his lawyer's business card, at the same time attempting to juggle his cell phone, and the manila envelope. Dropping the envelope to the ground Mike placed his foot on it to prevent it blowing away, and called his lawyer. Advising John that he had been served with a Divorce Decree, John asked him if he's read it. With a sheepish smile, Mike looked down at the envelope advised John that he was staring at it as they spoke.

"Well bring it by the office Mike, and I will look at it. In the meantime, I won't proceed with your decree as it may now be redundant."

Thanking John for his time, Mike agreed to swing by John's office in a day or two.

Bending down to retrieve the dis-tasteful envelope, Mike decided to head to Claude's Bistro right around the corner, where he could take a few minutes to assimilate this new development.

Entering Claude's, Mike was greeted by a bouquet of seductive aromas, causing his stomach to immediately begin growling in anticipation. The aroma of freshly brewed coffee, married with the mouthwatering scent of freshly baked croissants, bagels, and spicy, meat filled pastries was the reason Mike had visited Claude's regularly for the last three years.

SOLITARY TREE

Advancing towards the counter to place his order, Mike glanced into the glass display shelf to the left of the cash register, where Claude's delectable delicacies temporarily resided, before being purchased by discerning customers.

Nodding his head in greeting at the customers seated on the bright cherry red, vinyl covered swivel stools to his right, Mike spotted the formidable figure of Claude himself, emerge through the batwing style doors that led to the kitchen.

The massively built French Canadian expatriate with the severely crushed nose, the lifelong memento of some long-forgotten brawl, who surprisingly for such a large person possessed an incredibly mellifluous voice, insisted on personally greeting all his customers. Enquiring how Mike was today in his heavily accented patois, he asked Mike if he would like the usual. Spotting an empty booth in the far corner of the moderately sized room, Mike moved towards it passing by several patrons seated at booths that lined the inside wall, with tables placed along the outside wall looking onto the sidewalk. Seating himself, Mike threw the envelope onto the red and white checkered plastic table cloth, almost knocking over the old-fashioned sugar dispenser. Claude's Bistro was a study of a past generation, the glass sugar dispensers that you pour sugar out of, the black and white pictures of past and present Hockey players adorning the walls, and most importantly the personal touch, that has sadly been lost with most other businesses. Along with the incredible food, these were the reasons that had Mike returning to Claude's whenever he had the opportunity.

The young male food runner carefully placed Mike's steaming hot coffee, served in an old fashioned institutional white, hefty porcelain mug, along with a small plate that held a fresh, out of the oven sesame seed bagel, accompanied with a small dash of crème cheese, on the table, and wished Mike bon appetite.

SOLITARY TREE

Savoring the smell, Mike attacked the bagel with a vengeance, remembering too late as he burnt his fingertips that it had not had a chance to cool down.

Cursing silently, he blew on the offended fingertips attempting to ease the stinging sensation. This time exercising a degree of restraint, Mike gingerly picked up the bagel and took small cautionary bites to avoid burning his lips and mouth. Slowly sipping the last of his coffee, Mike removed the small notebook from his shirt pocket and reviewed his list of things to do. Looking up as the busboy approached to clear his dishes, Mike asked him if there was a phone directory he could use.

"I can go see, there should be one around here somewhere."

Returning shortly, he placed the voluminous directory in front of Mike and removed the empty plate.

Thanking the young man, Mike began flipping through it, jotting down several addresses in his note book.

Placing a tip under his coffee mug Mike rose from the booth, paid his bill and thanking Claude, Mike exited the Bistro and walked back towards the precinct to retrieve his vehicle.

Inside his vehicle, Mike checked his notebook to confirm an address then headed to his destination.

Upon entering the business that he was searching for, Mike heard the muted tinkle of the door chime announcing his entrance. Advancing through the bright, airy, fresh smelling office Mike made his way towards a counter with small sign proclaiming it to be the reception desk. Amusement at what he saw caused a glimmer of a smile to appear at the corner of his mouth. First it was his lawyer's receptionist Angela, who was busy with her fingernails, now this grandmotherly looking receptionist was studiously occupied with her knitting.

"Hello there, I'm looking for Frankie," enquired Mike.

As her rapidly moving knitting needles came to a halt, she looked up at Mike and informed him that she was Frankie.

"Oh, I'm sorry, given the type of business, I was sort of expecting a fat guy, with no hair, smoking a stinky cigar."

SOLITARY TREE

Rising from her chair, she placed the needles and the garment they were producing on a small table, then moved gracefully towards the counter, chuckling gently she informed Mike she hears that all the time.

"So, young man, what brings you to my office this fine day?"

Taking in the obviously expensive attire, the small round eye glasses perched on a button of a nose; the gray hair tied conservatively in a bun on the top of her head, Mike had some reservations concerning her ability to assist him.

Smiling at Mike she revealed a set of small, evenly spaced teeth.

"Let's start at the beginning shall we. Hi there, my name is Frankie and I am the owner and sole investigator of Frankie's Investigations." Extending her right hand towards Mike she asked. "And you are?"

Shaking the proffered hand Mike introduced himself.

Moving from behind the counter and joining Mike, she pointed towards a comfortable looking couch and suggested they sit and discuss Mike's needs. Seated on the couch, Frankie picked up a pen and note pad from the small coffee table and asked Mike to begin.

Still doubtful about Frankie's abilities to assist him, Mike attempted to think of a polite way to extricate himself from her office.

Rising from the couch, Frankie held up a hand towards Mike informing him she will be right back.

Returning to the couch with a black laptop computer, she smiled warmly at Mike and began to speak. "I know exactly what you're thinking. How can this grandmother possibly help me?" Pointing at the laptop computer she continued. "This is the world, with this I don't ever have to leave my office. There is nothing, or no one I can't find with this. So why don't you tell me what you are here for, and we will see what we can do."

SOLITARY TREE

Deciding that maybe she just might be able to help, Mike related to her what befell his daughters, and who the alleged abductors were purported to be.

Amazed as he watched Frankie's fingertips skip lightly across the keyboard with the same speed that she displayed while knitting, Mike was fascinated by the fact that before he was finished speaking he heard a copier begin to quietly whir behind the counter.

Rising gracefully from the couch, Frankie returned shortly with a sheaf of papers in her right hand, handing them wordlessly to Mike, he began to sift through them. Raising an eyebrow at Frankie in surprise, he recognized that a portion of the information she had accessed was purported to be inaccessible on the Police Department's internal server.

Exuding the same warm smile towards Mike, she watched him as he perused the information she had so quickly produced.

Looking up from reading, and matching Frankie's warm smile with one of his own, Mike asked her how much this was going to cost him to have her assist him in locating his children.

Issuing a low, throaty chuckle, Frankie assured Mike that he would be able to afford her services. "Since I do all my research right here, there are no expenses, and besides that Detective, I want to be able to re-unite you with your daughters."

Feeling a new-found respect and admiration for Frankie's obvious prowess, Mike continued to sift through the papers. Holding up one with the caption, "Human Trafficking" he asked Frankie if he could take this one with him.

With a twinkle in her eye she advised Mike that since he will be paying for them, he is entitled to take them all.

Enjoying a sense of cautious optimism that he had enlisted someone, who will employ a new direction in the search for his daughters, Mike soon took his leave.

Arriving back at his three-bedroom apartment, Mike began the most painful task he had assigned himself.

SOLITARY TREE

Entering the miniscule third bedroom, Mike rummaged through the closet until he located his old duffel bag. Traversing the narrow hallway into his bedroom, he began stuffing articles of clothing into the smelly duffel bag.

When he could no longer manage to squeeze any further clothes into it, he slid the throat of the bag closed along the tie strings and secured it with a granny knot.

Moving to the tiny safe kept with- in the confines of the closet, Mike opened it and removed the girl's personal identification information. These contained the girl's fingerprints, as well as records of their DNA markers, at the same securing his passport.

Entering what used to be the bedroom shared by his two daughters, Mike sat down on Alicia's bed, closed his eyes and released a heartfelt sigh, and for a few minutes pondered what might have been. Rising from the bed he moved to the four drawers stand up dresser upon which sat several pictures, Mike secured a picture of himself and the girls, then plucking a stuffed animal from each of the beds left the room without a backward glance.

Arriving in the kitchen Mike glanced around for a scrap of paper, finding a piece of white lined paper in the kitchen junk drawer, he used one of Alicia's bright red crayons to write a few words on it. With one last glance around the room Mike moved to the apartment door, leaving it ajar he taped the paper to the door with the words written on it "I'm done. Anything you want in here, help yourself." Making his way downstairs carrying the stuffed animals and his duffel bag, Mike went to the apartment manager's office and handing in his keys left the building.

CHAPTER FIVE

Seated in his car; Mike looked across the front seat at the ugly stuffed Giraffe that was Alicia's, and the stuffed Wiener dog that belonged to Desiree, and solemnly informed them that they are now persons with no fixed address. Deciding that for the foreseeable future they will be calling a Motel home, Mike started the car and began his search for accommodations. Having found what Mike thought to be a reasonably clean, and affordable motel, he lugged his meager belongings into the room. The stuffed giraffe and dog shared the one small bed, and Mike took ownership of the other small bed.

Flopping onto the bed, Mike fervently hoped that this was not the direction his life was going to take.

The sudden blast of a large truck's obnoxious horn woke Mike from a troubled slumber. Taking a minute to get his bearings and remember where he now lived, Mike rolled over, placing his feet on the cold, cracked, yellow linoleum covered floor. Shaking his head to clear the remaining cobwebs from his brain, he could recall vague, fog enshrouded fragments of the dream that had rapidly evolved into a nightmare. Rising he headed into the miniscule bathroom, turning on the shower he stepped in almost banging his head on the shower faucet that was obviously meant for people shorter than himself.

SOLITARY TREE

Sucking in a sudden deep breath as the jet of cold water stung his unsuspecting skin, Mike quickly opened the hot water tap as far as it would go. Shivering under the spray of cold water, Mike's patience was finally rewarded when the water temperature increased to what could barely be described as tepid. Grunting in disgust, Mike pushed aside the plastic flower covered shower curtain with such force, it separated from the curtain rod. Looking at the sodden mass that was now lying at his feet he unleashed a torrent of obscenities, which had nothing whatsoever to do with the fucked-up shower curtain, but more to do with the way his life had become irreversibly lost to him. All he ever wanted from life was a family, and a rewarding career, right now those two illusions were as fucked up as the hapless shower curtain. Wrapping the wet towel, he had dried himself with around his waist, Mike padded barefoot into the bedroom where he plucked his weapon from its holster and walked into the kitchen. Placing the weapon on the decrepit table, Mike leaned against the counter and stared at the weapon knowing that he could end this miserable existence in an instant. All it would require is one small effort, and he would never again suffer the pain of loss, as of this minute the desire to feel nothing is almost overwhelming. Finally, after a silent war with himself that lasted fully ten minutes, Mike reached over and picked up his weapon, staring at it he muttered. "Not yet."

Dressed, Mike returned to the kitchenette searching for a coffee machine, once he had the machine figured out, it soon began uttering sounds like it was working, leaning backwards against the counter Mike looked in disgust at his current lodgings. While the coffee machine happily gurgled, Mike became aware of a vile smell, lifting his arm he sniffed his armpit and was relieved to find out he was not the source of this smell. Now more curious then ever he began tracking this mal-odor with his nose.

SOLITARY TREE

Noticing that as he turned toward the miniscule sink it became significantly worse, Mike bent his head into the sink and taking a small sniff, realized that the odor was issuing from the sinks drain. No longer hearing the coffee machine gurgle and hiss, Mike poured the steaming contents into the lone, chipped blue porcelain mug. Taking a small tentative taste, Mike grimaced, muttering out loud. "Worst fuckin coffee I've ever had," tossing the mug and its contents into the sink in disgust.

Not sure why he thought this might be a place to temporarily call home, Mike collected his duffel bag, the two stuffed animals and left the premises. Emerging from the room, Mike was greeted with the cool damp air of an early March morning.

Throwing his belongings into his car, he walked briskly to the manager's office, placed the room key on the counter and informed the sleepy looking night manager he won't be back.

Knowing that he would be able to have a hot shower at the precinct, including the fact that his electric razor was there Mike headed to the precinct.

Seated in his new office at the precinct, having showered and shaved and sipping a hot coffee, Mike decided that he did not need to punish himself. His dream of a wife and family has headed in a direction that he never expected, but this was not caused by anything he had done. He did not need to debase himself as a form of punishment, he also came to terms with the fact that just because his wife Adele left the marriage, didn't make him a failure.

Feeling somewhat better about himself, Mike elected to begin the process of making this office his own. Returning to his old desk that he had shared with Larry, Mike placed his few personal items into a small box and carried them into his office.

Mounting the picture of himself and his daughters into the cheap gold frame he had bought, Mike placed it in the center of his desk. Gazing at a picture of himself and Adele laughing, Mike remembered the picture being taken in the dawn of their relationship.

SOLITARY TREE

That small window of carefree time they enjoyed before life, and all its demands took over. Resisting the temptation to bury it in the bottom drawer of the desk, Mike set it beside the one of him and the girls. "One big happy family," Mike stated sarcastically.

"I sincerely hope you're not going to answer yourself."

Glancing up in annoyance at this intrusion, Mike was astonished to see the gray haired, stately figure of the precinct captain lounging against his office door frame.

Standing up, Mike apologized profusely for not seeing him.

Waving his hand in the air dismissing Mike's apology, the captain went on to say that he had been advised that Mike was in his office and wanted to stop by.

Surprised that the captain would be aware of Mike's presence in the office at this early hour, the captain explained that there was not much his personal assistant Bowers was not aware of. Pointing to an empty chair he asked. "Mind if I sit down?"

"Of course, not sir."

"I sincerely appreciate the initiative you're displaying by being here already Mike. I believe you had requested several personal days and would not be here until Monday."

Not feeling the need to explain to the captain that it's because he had nowhere else to go that brought him here this morning, Mike smiled and thanked him.

The captain then quietly informed Mike that the team of Detectives tasked with investigating the shooting, had discovered a suicide note left by the young lady. He went on to explain that it appeared the young lady had suffered from serious mental health issues, and sadly, was not able to receive the help she so desperately needed.

Hearing that the young lady had chosen to end her life, did nothing to ease the distress Mike felt at having been the instrument of her demise.

SOLITARY TREE

 Mike thanked the captain for taking time from his busy schedule to inform him of these developments.
 "Well young man, I have a lot of confidence in your capabilities.
 Quite frankly, there were people who thought I was wrong to place you in this position as Chief of Detectives, they argued that you were too young, and do not have the wisdom acquired from years on the force. I have found that usually the people who complain the loudest, have an agenda of their own. I might encourage others to freely speak their minds, that doesn't mean that I have to agree with them."
 Watching the captain closely as he spoke, Mike could discern the cold, tempered steel that lay beneath the outwardly likeable persona the captain projected.
 "I want you to succeed Mike, there will be times when you and I will butt heads," shrugging his shoulders in resignation, added. "Unfortunately, it is the nature of the beast.
 Just remember that I know, you will always have the precinct's best interests at heart. Now young man, I have taken up enough of your time, I will let you get back to whatever it was you were doing."
 Rising from his chair Mike extended his right hand and firmly shook the captain's hand, thanking him again for taking the time from his busy schedule to inform him of the shooting investigation, as well as his confidence in Mike's ability to do the job.
 Mike's resolve to be successful was immeasurably strengthened by the captain's words. Understanding the best way for him to learn about the Detectives that now fell under his jurisdiction, would be to spend time with them on the streets. However, since that was not a viable option, the next best way was to study their personnel files. Moving to the battered, dark green, four drawers filing cabinet stuck in the corner behind his desk, Mike bent down to open the bottom drawer.

SOLITARY TREE

Surprised at how hard it was to open, he glanced at the side of the cabinet and seeing indentations, realized that the cabinet has borne the brunt of someone's anger. Exerting a large amount of force, Mike was finally able to open the bottom drawer, he was not at all surprised when he discovered a half full bottle of vodka, his surprise lay in the fact that the bottle still harbored a quantity of the fiery liquid. There had been rumors that his predecessor had enjoyed a fondness for alcohol, and had been caught several times stealing large sips by his subordinates. Jerking open the second drawer from the bottom, Mike found the elusive personnel files, placing the twenty-three copious files on his desk, he sat down and began thumbing through them.

Hearing a knock on his door, Mike glanced up to see the nattily dressed figure of Detective Hans Albright standing in the doorway.

"Morning Hans. What I can do for you?"

"Morning Mike, I was just wondering if you had a minute?"

"Of course, Come on in and sit down," invited Mike, pointing to an empty chair whilst discreetly closing the file he had been perusing.

Seating himself in the proffered chair, Hans crossed his legs and brushed away several invisible pieces of lint off his slacks, at the same time displaying well-manicured finger nails.

"Say Mike, I have been thinking you might need someone to be your second in command. Someone who could step in to your shoes if, or when you're tied up in meetings. Someone such as myself who has the knowledge and experience of how things are done around here."

Leaning back in his comfortable black leather, high backed chair, Mike sagaciously studied Hans while he was speaking. Absorbing the perfect hair, patrician nose, the glaringly white, even teeth, the word politician came to mind as he summed up Han's appearance.

SOLITARY TREE

"You're absolutely right Hans," agreed Mike affably. "I will need someone for those occasions when I can't be here."

Almost blinding Mike with his dazzling teeth, Hans was about to thank him for this opportunity when Mike continued. "I will certainly take what you have said here under advisement Hans, but I have yet to make a decision about who I will appoint as my surrogate."

With disappointment clearly etched across his frowning countenance, and much to Mike's annoyance, Hans continued to plead his case. Informing Mike that he was the only one who should possibly be considered as a candidate for Mike's surrogate, given his high percentage of solved crimes.

Mike's patience with this prima-Dona Detective was rapidly evaporating, and through gritted teeth re-iterated to him that when Mike had made his decision everyone will know.

Unwillingly to believe that he was not automatically Mike's obvious choice, Hans advised Mike in a clearly malevolent voice that he, Hans Albright should have been the new Chief of Detectives not Mike.

Albright even went so far as to suggest that perhaps Mike's appointment, was more about Mike representing a minority then it was about Mike's ability

Having had enough of Hans and his fucking white teeth, Mike ordered him to immediately vacate the office, failure to do so could result in disciplinary action.

Taking his time rising from the chair, Hans attempted to stare down Mike, failing that, with a scornful glare, he slowly left the office

"Jesus Christ, what an asshole," Mike swore out loud as he watched the receding back of Albright.

Hearing a muted beep from his desktop computer indicating incoming E-mail, Mike hit the enter button and was instantly inundated with E-mails.

SOLITARY TREE

There was a ten-page document pertaining to his office budget, another five-page document regarding unresolved outstanding personnel issues. Scanning the highlights of the E-mail regarding his office budget, Mike realized that he would be able to hire a secretary. Immediately the young lady with the Australian accent from the Police garage entered his thoughts.

Having met her only briefly several months ago, and given the circumstances of that meeting she might not be inclined to work for Mike. At the time, he had just been informed that a lady he thought of as a close friend, had been identified as the victim of a hit and run. In his haste to procure his Police vehicle and attend the scene, Mike, unable to locate his vehicle in the garage, had yelled at her venting his frustration, afterwards he realized that she had remained unflappable during Mike's tirade.

Exiting the E-mail program, Mike left his office closing the door behind him Mike headed to the stairwell, descending to the car garage where the patrol cars were parked and serviced. Locating the service manager's office Mike introduced himself and enquired about a young lady with an Australian accent.

"If you find someone with a clipboard out there, then you have found her," grunted the beleaguered looking service manager.

Leaving the manager to his chaos, Mike began wandering the brightly lit garage in search of an Australian girl. He did not have to go far before he spotted the lady of medium stature, writing notations on the ever-present clipboard.

"Excuse me Miss, you probably don't remember me," probed Mike.

"You're right."

"I am?" responded a puzzled Mike.

"Yes. I don't remember you," she remarked in soft voice couched lightly in an Australian accent.

Chuckling at her response, Mike then introduced himself, at the same time noting the short brunette hair, her luminous chestnut colored eyes, the slightly wider than normal mouth.

SOLITARY TREE

She reminded Mike that the last time they spoke he was in such a hurry that he was quite rude, and did not properly introduce himself, but since she was not one to hold a grudge she introduced herself as Yolanda Beggersly.

Shaking his head in amazement at her memory, Mike politely enquired if she had any office skills.

Yolanda informed Mike that she had graduated with honors in an Office Management curriculum, from a local Post Secondary Institution.

Displaying a timid smile, Mike congratulated her on her success, then explained to her that he was the new Chief of Detectives, and was in dire need of a secretary. With a small degree of trepidation, Mike asked her if she would consider coming to work for him.

Her next question caught Mike flatfooted. "What does the position pay?" enquired a serious looking Yolanda.

"Oh shit! I'm sorry I really don't know," responded Mike with a small measure of embarrassment. "But you will find out once you start going through all the budget information," returned Mike with a hopeful smile.

"Well it must pay more than this," with that said, she marched off to her manager's office, placed the clipboard on the counter and informed him that she had resigned.

The next two hours flew by, as the two of them planned for a new desk and computer to be set up for Yolanda.

Mike advised her that he needed to leave for a couple of appointments, but she was welcome to use his office computer to commence her duties as his new assistant. He then mentioned that he would be greatly indebted to her if she could find him some decent living quarters.

"What sort of place are you looking for? "enquired Yolanda.

Shrugging his shoulders Mike replied. "I don't know, something simple, clean and cheap."

Suddenly Yolanda realized who she was now working for. "You're the one whose kids were taken!"

SOLITARY TREE

"Yes, I am," Mike replied simply.

With burning cheeks, she exclaimed. "Oh, my god! I'm so sorry, I never realized it was you."

"That's alright, no reason to apologize, you couldn't have known," remarked an understanding Mike.

Gazing sympathetically at Mike, Yolanda bestowed a gentle squeeze to his arm, before heading into the office to begin her new career.

Extremely satisfied at the way his first unofficial day as the new Chief of Detectives had progressed, Mike allowed a small smile to play at the corner of his lips.

Arriving at the law office of Lynch and Associates, Mike entered the office and moved towards the counter. He was surprised to see the receptionist Angela, not immersed in the arduous work of performing a manicure. Projecting a professional demeanor, she asked Mike to follow her, knocking on the door she waited for a response from within. Granted permission to enter she opened the door and announced to her employer that Mike Chance had arrived. Ushering Mike into the large room, she smoothly backed out and quietly closed the door.

Shaking his head in amazement at the transformation in Angela, Mike looked towards John who had rounded his large oaken desk and with hand extended welcomed Mike.

"I know, it's uncanny," mused a smiling John. "All I had to do was mention the fact that I had an interview planned for an office manager, and it's like a new Angela. appeared. Just wish I had thought about doing that a while ago," chuckling softly. "Anyways, that's not why you're here, do you have the envelope?" enquired John.

Handing him the manila envelope containing the Divorce Decree, John invited him to sit down and make himself comfortable while he took a quick look.

Twenty-five minutes later Mike finally heard John issue a small grunt of surprise. "Well Mike, this looks like the standard, run of the mill quickie divorce settlement.

SOLITARY TREE

 But, what I do find alarming is there is no mention of your shared children. There is absolutely nothing in here about shared custody, or full custody in the event the girls are located. You did say you have two daughters, did you not."

 Mike then related to John, his recent phone call to his estranged wife Adele, apprising John that Adele cannot, and will not, spend her life searching for something that had been lost. As he re-counted the phone call to John, it pained Mike greatly to realize that the woman he had once loved, turned out to be someone he never knew.

"Yes Mike, we human beings are a fickle bunch," agreed John studying the document as he continued speaking. "It would appear to me that she has relinquished any custodial rights she may have regarding the girls. As your legal representative I, would not have a problem with you signing this document. She is also not challenging you for any shared material goods that you may have accrued during your married years."

 "That's good news," chortled Mike. "I gave everything away except for two stuffed animals."

 Chuckling at this little tidbit of information, John surmised out loud. "What Adele doesn't know, probably won't hurt her.

 I will be adding an in-depth codicil to this document. We need to protect your interests where the girls are concerned.

 If she has indeed relinquished her rights, then she needs to recognize the fact that this document cannot be rescinded on a whim." Consulting his desk calendar, John advised Mike that he will have the document ready for a signature by Tuesday next week.

"Sounds good John," commented Mike rising from his chair shaking John's warm, dry, hand in farewell. Making his way past the receptionist desk, Mike heard Angela bid him a good day.

 Seeing his elongated shadow pre-cede him down the sidewalk, and feeling a chill in the early March air, checking his watch Mike was surprised to see it was already four-thirty p.m.

SOLITARY TREE

What should have been a quick twenty-minute drive back to the precinct, quickly turned into a fifty-minute ordeal, strident vehicle horns blaring, as drivers, impatient with the sluggish pace vehicles were moving, wrongly thought that blasting horns would expedite the process.

Entering the precinct Mike nodded his head in the direction of several acquaintances, and waved at a few others before making his way to the stairwell. Reaching the second-floor Detectives room, Mike was surprised at the changes that had occurred in his brief absence. Yolanda's desk had been placed directly in front of his office, the medium sized, dark colored desk was already home to a pair of computer monitors, situated side by side like mute twins. Mike scowled when he noticed Detective Hans Albright lounging against the outer wall of his office, and who appeared to be engaged in a serious conversation with Yolanda.

Nodding his head curtly at Albright, Mike turned his attention to Yolanda, commenting that he was surprised to see she was still working.

Realizing that Mike was completely ignoring him, Albright advised Yolanda to keep it in mind, with a baleful at Mike, walked briskly to his desk.

Staring at the retreating back of Albright, Yolanda commented drily. "That guy is an asshole! Ten minutes after you left, he was informing me that he should be the new Chief of Detectives, and that I should be working for him. That you only have the position because the Captain bowed to pressure over placing minorities' in senior management positions."

Turning his head towards the seated Albright, Mike's black eyes flashed with anger at the man's conceit, returning his gaze to Yolanda, Mike advised her to ignore the pompous asshole.

"Oh, before I forget," Yolanda handed Mike a page torn from her notebook. "This is the address to your new residence."

Looking curiously at the page, then smiling at his beaming secretary, asked her how she knew he would even like the place.

SOLITARY TREE

"Oh, you will love it," she stated unequivocally. "The lady I was speaking with sounded lovely.

It is a self-contained basement suite. You will have your own entryway and a place to park your car," concluded a smiling Yolanda, proud of her success.

Looking closer at the address, Mike enquired where it was located.

With her mouth smiling widely, displaying small evenly spaced teeth, she informed Mike that since he's the detective, he should be able to locate the residence.

Smiling at this minor taunt, Mike commented nonchalantly. "Please don't take this the wrong way Yolanda, I was going to grab a burger at the fast food place just down the street, I wonder if you would like to join me?"

"I won't take it the wrong way, and yes I'm famished, so I accept your kind invitation."

While Yolanda logged off her computer Mike slipped into his office, turned off the lights, then closed and locked his door. Making their way towards the stairwell, they were blissfully unaware of the malevolent look Albright threw in their direction.

Seated at the small table, in the crowded and noisy fast food eatery, with discarded wrappers from the hamburgers, and a few greasy, stray French Fries scattered on the plastic tray, Mike asked Yolanda why she was working in the garage when she had a degree in office management.

A frustrated Yolanda informed Mike that being young, and female seemed to work against her. She had applied at many different offices, and was told that with no actual experience in an office environment they unfortunately couldn't hire her. She asked these same Human Resources managers how she would be able to obtain experience, if she was unable to secure a position. She went on to say that they would shrug their shoulders helplessly, apologize, explain their hands were tied, adding when she had acquired some experience please by all means re-apply.

SOLITARY TREE

"Well their loss is my gain," commented Mike. "Now I better go find those new accommodations that my secretary has found for me. Can I drop you somewhere?" enquired Mike.

Thanking Mike for the burger, Yolanda assured him that there's a bus stop outside the precinct that she uses all the time.

"Okay, we will see you tomorrow. "remarked Mike picking up both their plastic trays, emptying them into the yellow and red garbage receptacles, which were strategically placed by the exit.

It took twenty-five minutes for Mike to locate the address that Yolanda had written on the note paper, though it was already dusk of an early March evening, Mike could clearly see that each house's domain was protected by tall green hedges.

Parking his car on the street in front of the address of the address written on the note paper, Mike walked the short distance in the cool evening air to the front door with a large black welcome mat placed directly in front of the door. Knocking on the door, Mike respectfully stepped back from the door, in an unconscious move to demonstrate that he was not being aggressive. Bathed in the sudden illumination of the porch light, Mike watched as the door opened the three inches permitted by the safety chain, followed closely by an elderly gentleman demanding to know what he wanted.

Apologizing for the late hour Mike held up his police issued identification for the homeowner's scrutiny, explaining that his secretary had called them on his behalf about a basement suite for rent.

Through the small opening permitted by the door's safety chain, the home owner judiciously studied Mike's identification, grunting his acceptance the door suddenly closed, then just as quickly re-opened in its entirety. Inviting Mike into the house, the elderly, stooped, frail looking gentleman leaning on a wooden cane, was joined in the small foyer by a handsome looking, slightly overweight lady.

SOLITARY TREE

Once again introducing himself, Mike learned that his potential landlords were Fred and Janine Willoby.

With the introductions completed, the frail looking Fred apologized, explaining that since he was not as mobile as he once was he will return to the Livingroom, and that Janine would show Mike the suite. Ushering Mike into the cozy, warm kitchen with walls adorned by mementos and pictures that depicted their many years together, Janine asked Mike to have a seat while she waited as the chocolate chip, banana muffins she had in the oven were just about ready to come out. Absorbing the ambiance of the kitchen, the savory aroma of the muffins baking in the oven, Mike's already convinced that Yolanda had found exactly what he had been looking for.

Slipping on a pair of flower printed oven mitts, the handsome looking Janine, with her stylishly short, well-groomed gray hair, carefully removed the pan bearing the steaming muffins from the hot oven, and placed it gently onto a metal rack to begin the cooling process.

Thanking Mike for his patience, she then gave him a tour of the basement suite with the aroma of the freshly baked muffins pursuing them. The suite was everything Mike could have hoped for; he was pleasantly surprised to discover the height of the ceiling in the suite was more than enough to accommodate his six feet three inches.

The already furnished suite, with walls painted in soft pastel colors would suit Mike's needs perfectly. Looking up at Mike, Janine asked him what he thought, Mike enthusiastically informed her that it was perfect. Smiling at his enthusiasm they made their way back upstairs, and joined the waiting Fred in the large spacious Livingroom.

Beckoning towards the much used, comfortable looking couch, Janine invited Mike to seat himself, enquiring if they would like a tea and muffin.

SOLITARY TREE

Both men graciously accepted her offer, advising them she will be back shortly she headed towards the kitchen, in the meantime, Mike and Fred sat in companionable silence watching the Basketball game on the large flat screen television.

True to her word Janine returned shortly bearing what looked like an antique silver serving tray, on which rested an equally antique tea pot, there was also a small plate with several muffins cut in half, and coated with a generous slathering of melted butter. Picking up the television's remote control, from Fred's scuffed, brown leather ottoman, Janine with a pointed glance at the two men, turned the television off. With a cup of tea, and muffin in front of them, the three briefly discussed the upcoming presidential election as they inconspicuously sized each other up, with Fred announcing that as far as he was concerned all politicians were crooked.

Gently shushing her husband, Janine explained to Mike what they would charge him for rent, at the same time extending an open invitation to join them any time for supper.

Respectfully waiting for his wife to finish, Fred then entered the conversation, with a rasping voice he explained to Mike that since they were on a fixed income, they have had to begin garnering the extra income provided by renting the basement suite.

With a small smile, he jokingly mentioned that renting it to a cop would make them feel safe.

Janine then asked Mike if he would like to rent the suite, and if so when would he like to move in.

Swallowing the last bite of the delicious muffin, Mike thanked Janine for the wonderful treat, then stated "If it's alright with you folks, I would move in tonight."

"Really! You would like to move in tonight?" asked an incredulous Janine.

"I have a duffel bag with my clothes, and two small stuffed animals," declared Mike.

SOLITARY TREE

Looking as though she wanted to ask him about his lack of belongings, Fred spoke up and quietly told his wife that it was none of their business.

Not wanting to explain right now to this nice couple about what had befallen him, yet at the same wanting to assure them that he was trustworthy, Mike simply informed them that it's complicated, but one day he might be able to tell them.

"Well I don't think we have a problem with that," asserted Fred with a pointed look at his wife.

Looking first to her husband then to Mike, Janine smiled and welcomed Mike to their home.

CHAPTER SIX

At seven-fifteen Monday morning, Mike began his first official day at the twelfth precinct as the new Chief of Detectives. His toffee colored skin, a legacy from his ancestors, was still smarting from a close shave and liberal dousing of cologne, he had donned a pair of dark gray slacks, a powder blue colored shirt, and matching tie. Leaning up against his office door gazing out into the large, empty Detectives squad room, he attempted to shake off a feeling of melancholy, he was about to embark on a new career path as Chief of Detectives, and he had absolutely no one to celebrate this promotion with. Hearing the door at the head of the stairs open, Mike was not at all surprised to see the enterprising Yolanda walk briskly through the swinging doors, and head in his direction through the empty room.

Walking up to Mike she brazenly eyed him from head to toe. "Jesus Mike, dressed like that I know some of those female Detectives will want to take you home, and introduce you to their mothers as their new boyfriend," adding with a mischievous smile. "Perhaps even some of the male Detectives."

Smiling at her capriciousness Mike wished her good morning and was about to head into his office, when she held up her hand to stop him.

Pointing at his tie, she moved closer, reached up and with a couple of gentle tugs straightened it.

SOLITARY TREE

Thanking her, Mike sauntered into his office, sitting at his desk, he reached for the pad of legal sized paper and began to think of what he might say at his inaugural eight o'clock briefing. Lost in thought he heard an unobtrusive knock on his door, looking up he noticed Yolanda pointing at her watch.

Cursing silently, he ripped the paper from the pad and headed out into the now noisy squad room. Walking past Yolanda's desk, he swore he heard her say. "Break a leg."

Striding towards the head of the spacious room where a small podium was in front of the wall sized chalk board, Mike heard a jeering voice ridicule him about being late. Looking towards the voice, Mike was not surprised to see Detective Hans Albright near where he thought the voice originated from.

Reaching the podium Mike placed his piece of paper on it and smoothed it out, looking up at the twenty Detectives that now fell under his jurisdiction Mike suddenly felt overwhelmed. Dropping his gaze back to the paper Mike picked it up, crumpled it into a ball and threw it towards the brown garbage can in the corner. Leaving the podium, the assembled detectives watched with curiosity as he hooked a wooden backed chair from the front row, spun it backwards and sat down, this action was greeted with laughter and a smattering of applause.

"No one likes a speech and they like the speech giver even less," pronounced Mike. "Good Morning everyone. I trust everyone here knows me, if not check with Albright, I suspect he has a special name for me. The captain's mandate is to usher in a new era of police work." With both arms folded comfortably across the back of the chair Mike continued to inform his squad of what he would like to accomplish. He informed them that his office door will always be open, that he will catch as many cases as time allows. He would also like to initiate voluntary weekly information sessions, regarding ongoing cases.

SOLITARY TREE

Rising smoothly from his chair, Mike retrieved his cell phone from his front pants pocket, holding it aloft for all to see. "We all have one of these," he declared loudly.

"So, does everyone else outside of this office. Everyone who has one of these also has a camera, and video capabilities. Try to remember this people, you are being always watched by both the good guys as well as the bad. Believe me when I say, you don't want to see yourself on the six o'clock news, in the starring role on some disgruntled citizens video," allowing his eyes to rest on every person in the room whilst stating this new fact of life. Mike then apologized for keeping them so long and asked if anyone had a question. When no questions were forthcoming, Mike thanked them for their time and dismissed them.

Immensely relieved at having his first briefing under his belt, Mike moved towards the desk occupied by Herman Diaz.

"Morning Herman, how are you?" quizzed Mike.

"Morning yourself Mike. Doing just fine, thanks for asking," returned a cautious Herman, extremely conscious of the fact that he had been tasked with interviewing Mike over the shooting of the young lady.

"I have some urgent business I need to take of right now, would you be able to meet with me this afternoon?" probed Mike.

Locking eyes with his new boss, Herman acknowledged that he would be available later this afternoon.

"Thank-you Herman, we'll get together later today."

Back in his office, Mike had barely sat down, when he heard Yolanda subtly clearing her throat. Once she had Mike's attention she entered the office and tossed a familiar looking ball of crumpled paper onto his desk. With a broad smile, she pointed to the paper and shaking her head in admiration, informed Mike that he was good. "There is nothing written on that paper Mike, no speech, not even a pen mark."

Shrugging his shoulders helplessly at being caught out, he smiled sheepishly and with a knowing wink directed at her, admitted he hadn't known if it would work or not.

SOLITARY TREE

Pushing aside their shared moment of levity, Mike informed Yolanda that he will be out of the office for a couple of hours.

He had some urgent business to attend to, if something drastic should happen please contact him on his cell phone.

Parking his car in China town, Mike was fully aware that this next step in his quest to find his daughters, would likely be fraught with danger. Knowing that he had been under Ki Chiang Yee's surveillance almost the instant he left his car, Mike attempted to exude a casual ambiance, despite the apprehension he was experiencing as he walked toward his uninvited meeting with Ki Chiang Yee. Ki is the reputed head of the Chinese Tong, a well-organized and deadly crime syndicate. Mike's father had on many occasions impressed upon Mike, that although Ki was Mike's uncle, he was not to be trifled with, comparing Ki to a hunting Bengal Tiger, when you see the tiger it's too late, you are dead. Walking down a flight of stairs, Mike knocked loudly on a door that had been alleged to be able to easily withstand the impact of rocket propelled grenades. As the door opened he was grabbed roughly on both arms, and instantly propelled into a concrete wall's skin abrading surface. Unable to fight back even if he were so inclined, Mike submitted to the rough search for weapons. Removing Mike's weapon from its holster, the pair of massive Asians, obviously, twins, and dressed in of all things tuxedos, allowed Mike to remove his face from the dusty cement wall and turn to face them. The one on Mike's left who bore an impressive, angry looking scar running downwards from his left earlobe and disappeared under his chin, stepped towards Mike and gently brushed dust from his jacket. Meanwhile the bruiser to the right of Mike, moved a short distance away, spinning a dial on a medium sized wall safe deposited Mike's weapon inside, closing the door he gave the dial a quick spin. Then pushing a button on an intercom system hidden to most people's eyes spoke rapidly in what sounded to Mike like Cantonese. With his ear cocked towards the box, he received a reply almost immediately.

SOLITARY TREE

With Scarface leading the way, and his fellow body guard falling in behind Mike, they proceeded down the narrow, well-lit hallway. Arriving at what appeared to be a dead end, Mike was surprised when Scarface gently pushed on the wall and a large door silently opened.

Moving through the doorway, Mike was astounded to note the door was at least eight inches thick, he had been told this place was a fortress, the people that had told him this hadn't lied.

The large, cavernous room that Mike found himself in, was completely devoid of all furniture except for a chair placed in the center of the room. Indicating that Mike was to proceed towards the chair, Scarface and his partner crossed their arms across their massive chests, and became expressionless statues.

Walking towards the chair Mike realized that this was no ordinary chair, it was resplendent with ornate carvings, covered in what looked to be swatches of red and black satin, this chair was so large it could easily accommodate the bulk of someone weighing four hundred pounds, not the mere one hundred and eighty pounds of the person currently occupying it. This was a chair designed to be sat in by a Khan, the ferocious Mongol warlords of past centuries, this chair though, was unfortunately occupied by none other than Ki Chiang Yee.

Studying the gentleman occupying the chair, Mike knew Ki to be at least fifty years old, yet his face was that of someone half that age. Even though Ki was seated in the chair Mike could tell that he was almost as tall as Mike, with the same muscular build.

The lithe figure of Ki rose from the chair, dressed in a three-piece suit constructed from some of the finest Italian silk and was obviously tailored to fit him, he quickly closed the ten paces between himself and Mike. Watching the easy way that Ki moved, Mike was not surprised that his father compared Ki to a tiger.

Placing two large powerful hands on Mike's shoulders, Ki who was only two inches shorter than Mike, stared at him for a full minute before speaking. "Hello Mike."

SOLITARY TREE

"Hello Ki," answered Mike somberly, staring into his uncle's black fathomless eyes that harbored not a single shred of warmth whatsoever.

"It's been quite a few years."

"Yes, it has," agreed Mike non-committedly, adding "By coming here I have broken a promise I made to someone that I cherished dearly."

"And who might that someone be?" questioned Ki.

"My father!" declared Mike.

"Oh, yes your father."

"Ya you know, the guy whose funeral you chose not to attend," growled Mike.

"I did not want to insult my brother by attending his funeral, he would not have wanted me there," argued Ki.

"Personally, I don't give a rat's ass what you think, that's not the reason I'm here," rumbled Mike.

Closing his eyes Ki seemed to ponder Mike's statement, musing out loud. "What could possibly motivate a son to break a promise to his deceased father?" Then as though the answer was written on the inside of his eyelids, he triumphantly asked Mike if he was here seeking help in the search for his girls.

"You know what happened to my daughters?" questioned Mike.

"Jesus Mike," expostulated Ki angrily. "Of course, I do, you were crying on network television, I have never seen anything quite so embarrassing. Instead of crying on national television like a young kid who had stubbed his toe, you should have been out hunting the fucking people that committed the crime," snorted a disgusted Ki.

Admitting to Ki that he had exhausted all means at his disposal to find his girls, he was indeed here seeking assistance. Mike also informed Ki that he was searching for the people responsible for his girl's abduction.

Returning to his chair, Ki questioned Mike about these other people.

SOLITARY TREE

"Gwyn O'Mallory, Ellen Delveccio, and Larry Donovan," answered Mike

"Interesting group of people. Two crooked cops and a lady," murmured Ki.

"You knew that O'Mallory and Donovan were cops?" asked a puzzled Mike.

  Ki informed Mike in a voice carved from ice, that information is like currency, the more you have, the more powerful you are. In fact, he had also been looking for Gwyn O'Mallory, and would be very happy to locate him as there is an outstanding debt owed to Ki by O'Mallory.

With eyes like black obsidian reflecting the light in the room, Ki stared malevolently at Mike as though to intimidate him, returning the stare Mike asked Ki if he would be willing to help.

"You need to embrace your heritage Mike. You should re-claim your grandfather's family name, not this atrocity of a name that you now use. Our ancestors took what they wanted, anyone who stood in their way disappeared along with their families, and their names were never spoken again. If you were to act in this way people would have respected you, and not taken your property in the first place. You have allowed the laws of others to handcuff you, these laws that you have chosen to uphold have made you weak!" declared Ki with violent passion.

 Observing Ki's flared nostrils, and the demonic look in his uncle's eyes, Mike heatedly declared. "My father was right, you're fucking delusional, my daughters are not property; they are much more than that, they are my life. The reason we have laws, is to prevent assholes like you who prefer anarchy to an ordered society, so you can perpetuate your crimes against those who are unable to defend themselves.

"Do not come in to my home and dis-respect me!" bellowed an enraged Ki.

Shaking his head in disbelief, Mike turned and started walking towards Scarface and his twin.

SOLITARY TREE

"Michael!" bellowed the still enraged Ki. "Do not be foolish enough to presume that since we share blood, you will be safe here. You are a cop! That makes you my enemy, and a threat to my existence. Do not be so bold as to show up again without an invitation," cautioned Ki.

Coming to a halt, Mike refused to look back at his uncle during this tirade, when his uncle had finished, Mike who was staring at the waiting body guards asked Ki if he would help.

"I will see what I can do, I make no promises," declared a somewhat mollified Ki.

Lifting an arm up in a backwards wave, Mike quietly thanked his uncle and was escorted out of Ki's presence by Scarface and his partner. As Mike was about to step outside he was halted by Scarface, who reunited Mike with his weapon then holding up a cell phone for display he slid it into Mike's jacket pocket, and warned Mike the next time he wanted to talk to Ki, call the pre-set number on the phone.

Safely ensconced in his vehicle, with the phone stashed in his consul, Mike knew that Ki would at some future time exact his pound of flesh from Mike, the mere fact that Mike approached Ki meant a debt was owed. This is the world that Ki lived and flourished in, and the world that Mike now found himself a part of.

Back in his office, Mike began familiarizing himself with the apparently endless mountain of paperwork associated with his new command. Hearing a knock on the door, Mike looked up to see Herman Diaz standing in the doorway, with a sigh of relief, he pushed the small mountain of paperwork to the left side of his desk, standing up invited Herman to come in and sit down.

Not displaying any trace of emotion on his leathery face, Herman leaned back in the chair and asked Mike what it was he wanted.

"I would like to ask you if you would be interested in being my Deputy Chief? There will be times that I will be hung up in meetings or otherwise unavailable, I need to have someone that I trust implicitly to stand-in for me."

SOLITARY TREE

"Are you sure you have the right fellow in here?" drawled Diaz. "Albright has been telling anyone who will listen that he's the perfect choice for the position."

"Yes, that does not surprise me in the least," commented Mike. "If I was to appoint him as my Deputy, it would demonstrate a serious lack of judgement on my be-half. He is a pompous, conceited, windbag who in my estimation would be the worst possible choice. The captain has given me complete autonomy with respect to this office, and I would be honored if you would accept this appointment."

With a ghost of a smile, Diaz informed Mike that considering the interview regarding the death of the young female, he was amazed that he was being offered this position.

"It's precisely because of that interview that I am presenting this offer to you. I really like what you said about following the book. That is the type of person I am looking for."

"I appreciate the offer Mike, and gladly accept." professed a smiling Diaz.

Matching Diaz's smile with one of his own, Mike thanked him profusely and shaking Diaz's hand informed him they will get together in a few days to work out the details.

Watching Diaz walk towards his desk; Mike was pleased to know he will have an excellent deputy to work with.

Walking the few steps to Yolanda's desk, he watched in amazement as her fingertips danced across her keyboard, barely coming to rest before they flitted to the next key, sensing a presence close by, her fingers became immobilized as she looked up at Mike, who quietly asked her to locate a wheelchair for him.

Standing up she walked around her desk to inspect Mike's legs.

"Well looks like both your legs are still there, and I see no outward evidence of a broken leg, so I'm a little confused regarding your request for a wheelchair," she concluded with a clever little smile.

SOLITARY TREE

Chuckling at her astute detective work, Mike informed her that it's not for him, he explained that it just needed to be a simple type. It didn't need to be motorized, the person that he would like it for, has some mobility issues that a wheelchair would solve.

In less than an hour Yolanda reported to her boss that there would be a wheel chair waiting for him on the main floor of the precinct at precisely five p.m.

Shaking his head in admiration at her proficiency, Mike thanked her. Placing a call to his good friend Gary, he asked if they still played Basketball Monday nights at Jefferson High School, Gary advised Mike that the game starts at eight p.m. Thanking him Mike informed him that he might see him there.

A short time later, Mike glancing at his watch realized it's already after five, rising from his chair and stretching Mike exited his office. Seeing Yolanda still busy at her desk he insisted that she leave, as the work will still be there tomorrow, smiling at Mike she stated that she would be right behind him.

Arriving at his vehicle with the wheel chair, Mike tried to figure out how to get the wheel chair to fold so that it would fit into his car, quickly becoming annoyed at his lack of success he finally discovered a lever on the side and pulling lightly on it, the stubborn chair finally capitulated and folded up.

Parking his car in his landlord's driveway, Mike unloaded the wheel chair and pushed it to the front door. Making his way through his own entryway into the house Mike, knocked on the door that separated his basement suite and the house proper. Hearing Janine invite him to come in, Mike headed to the kitchen and outlined to her, his plan for Fred. At first Janine was somewhat dubious of Mike's plan, considering Fred's physical state, Mike however was not to be deterred, and was able to persuade Janine that Fred would be just fine.

SOLITARY TREE

With both parties wearing large smiles, they made their way into the Livingroom where Fred was watching his perennial Basketball game on the television, from the comfort of his recliner.

Looking first to his smiling wife, then at Mike, Fred asked them. "What's going on, why are you guys smiling like that?" adding. "Should I be worried?" with a smile of his own.

Moving to the front door Mike opened it and retrieved the waiting wheel chair, pushing it into the Livingroom Mike announced to the surprised Fred that going forward, Monday nights will be boy's night out.

The evening went far better than any expectations Mike may have entertained, first, going to a fast food joint where they ordered a deluxe cheese burger and French fries. The burger came complete with fried onions, mushrooms, along with every type of popular condiment, and a generous helping of grease. The French Fries were buried under a layer of delicious gravy and melted parmesan cheese, though only able to consume half of his burger, along with a few French fries, the twinkle in Fred's eyes, and the satisfied belch he discharged were more than enough reward for Mike.

The next stop was Jefferson High School, entering the acoustically challenged gymnasium, they were met with shrieks of protest produced by the soles of running shoes at the sudden starts and stops demanded of them, by the players wearing them.

The next hour flew by as Fred sat in his wheel chair and watched the game from the sidelines, clapping his hands enthusiastically as each team scored a basket, though unable to emit much more than a muted cheer, Fred's enjoyment was undeniably etched on his face.

Watching Fred become completely enraptured by the game, Mike fervently wished he could have shared moments like this with his own father. Joined on the bleachers by his good friend Gary, they caught up on each other's lives while watching the game. "Who's the guy in the chair?" asked Gary.

SOLITARY TREE

Mike explained to Gary who Fred was, and why he had brought him here. After the game, Mike, and Gary were delighted to watch an ecstatic Fred clap his hands in appreciation of the player's efforts. Without speaking, Gary rose from his perch beside Mike, and quickly descended from the bleachers approaching the assembled players from both teams as they congratulated each other. Emerging shortly from the tightly grouped players, Gary carried the game ball over to Fred and offered it to him, complete with all the players signatures. As Mike watched this unfold, he was touched by both his friend's ability to care about others, as well as Fred's tearful acceptance of the game ball.

This night out was such a resounding success, that every succeeding Monday night Basketball game was witnessed by Fred sitting in his wheel chair, from his favorite spot on the sidelines.

CHAPTER SEVEN

Dreading the approaching month of May, for with it came the realization that a year had passed since he had last seen his daughters though he knew his search would never cease, Mike's optimism for being reunited with them has waned.

On a quiet mid-morning weekday, Mike was surprised to hear an angry Yolanda shout. "Hey! You can't just walk in there!"

Looking up at this sudden outburst Mike was surprised to see three large burly men enter his office, the last of the trio to enter Mike's office turned back towards the angry Yolanda, and with a look that left Yolanda feeling like she had been violated, told her not to get her underwear in a knot, then with a smirk closed the door behind him and leaned his broad back against it.

Mike watched with curiosity tinged with contempt, as the other two without any invitation from Mike sat themselves down. Reading the badges prominently displayed on their jackets, Mike ascertained that these three men were from the Federal Police Agency. The one seated to Mike's left threw a yellow manila envelope onto Mike's desk, at the same time attempted to stare Mike into a subservient posture.

Looking at the manila envelope lying on his desk, Mike to the consternation of the three men broke into loud and boisterous laughter. Wiping away imaginary tears of jocularity, Mike informed the trio in a voice that conveyed his contempt for them, that the last time he received a manila envelope like that, it was from his wife's lawyer announcing she wanted a divorce.

In a sudden about face Mike's dark and forbidding countenance displayed the ridicule he felt for these three intruders.

SOLITARY TREE

"You guys really need to change your training manual," barked Mike scornfully. "You think you three men, pardon me, two men and your human fuckin door stop, can come into my office and intimidate me!" blazed Mike thoroughly pissed off at this unannounced intrusion.

"We're Feds, you can't talk to us like that!" protested the doorstop.

"Actually, you're fucking lucky I haven't physically thrown you out of my office!" threatened Mike.

"Why don't you look at what's in the envelope?" quietly suggested the agent seated in the right-hand chair.

Knowing full well what's contained in the envelope, Mike wondered why it's taken this long to get a visit from the feds. The security cameras that Ki had protecting him, was equaled by the feds as they attempted to identify people as they arrived at Ki's place of business. Steeling himself Mike removed the eight by ten inch glossy pictures of himself entering, then later exiting Ki's place. Seeming to study the pictures Mike commented sarcastically. "Trust you guys to take a picture when my hair was mussed up, way to go."

"Hey asshole, we have you on fuckin film, entering and exiting the premises of a known gangster. Are you another fuckin dirty local cop?" barked the doorstop.

"Hank! That's enough!" admonished the more reasonable agent seated to Mike's right. "So, Mike, you have to admit that from our perspective you being seen at Ki's does raise some questions."

Looking at the agent's identification Mike asked if his name was pronounced Armon.

Nodding his head in the affirmative added. "The family name is Armon, my given name is Grant."

SOLITARY TREE

"Very well Grant. First off I owe you no explanation at all about my presence at Ki's. I don't give a rat's ass about what questions you may or may not have." With his mind flashing through various scenarios Mike decided to drop a bomb, knowing full well that despite their famed ineptness they would eventually stumble onto the fact regarding his familial ties to Ki. "Ki is my deceased father's older brother. I went there to call him an asshole for failing to attend his brother's funeral."

Mike almost laughed out loud, as the three men's jaws dropped open as the information he had just divulged sank in.

Sitting forward in his chair, Grant was almost beside himself with glee. "You're our man!" he exclaimed exultantly. "Ki is your uncle," Grant almost groaned out loud with orgasmic pleasure picturing himself being the agent that finally dethroned Ki, and the recognition that would bring. "We have been attempting for years to get someone inside Ki's organization, every time we have tried, our guy ends up dead."

"Don't think for a minute that I'm your guy," declared Mike vehemently. "The last time I had laid eyes on Ki I was eight years old. As I stated, the only reason I went there was to tell him he's an asshole. He would have no problem killing me as quickly as the next guy, he just happens to be an Uncle by an accident of birth. Now unless you asshole's happen to have a warrant in your fancy suits you can get the hell out of my office." Standing up he physically ushered the protesting trio from his office. Striking with the speed and deadly intent of a King Cobra, Mike struck out at the agent who had mouthed off to Yolanda. Grabbing a handful of the man's tie, Mike quickly revolved his wrist until his wrist was tight against the agent's throat. Slamming the agent up against the wall hard enough to make it shake, Mike then pressed his large, powerful forearm against the agent's throat.

SOLITARY TREE

With the agent now fully incapacitated, Mike's black eyes were radiating with his anger, warning the agent through gritted teeth. "That any time he felt tough enough to go against Mike then he was welcome to try. In the future, however, he will watch how he addressed Mike's assistant Yolanda, who he will now apologize to for his earlier behavior."

With the agent's face rapidly turning blue while Mike spoke, he hurriedly nodded his head in assent.

Releasing the man Mike was gratified when he heard the painful sounding, wheezing intake of air as the agent was finally able to breathe again, Mike added insult to injury by taking pains to straighten the man's tie.

As Mike looked over at the man's companions, they shrugged their shoulders in resignation. "He's an idiot," confirmed Grant.

Hearing the man continue to wheeze as he apologized to Yolanda, caused a smile to appear on Mike's face. Watching the backs of the departing trio Mike knew they would return at some point in time.

"Jesus Christ!" breathed Yolanda looking at her boss with amazement. "Remind me never to piss you off."

Smiling broadly at her, Mike advised Yolanda that right now might not be a good time to ask for a raise.

Laughing out loud at this wry comment, Yolanda agreed and informed Mike she would wait until next week.

Turning towards Herman Diaz's desk, Mike heard what sounded like a single person clapping, which then quickly turn into a crescendo of applause from the gathered detectives. Bowing slightly to his appreciative audience, Mike gestured for Herman to join him in his office. As Herman joined him, Mike asked him to please close the door, and grab a chair.

SOLITARY TREE

Although wondering what the hell had just occurred, Herman maintained a reserved silence while waiting for Mike to collect his thoughts.

Fanning the four, eight by ten inch glossy pictures in front of Herman, Mike explained where they were taken, and how it happened that Mike was photographed entering the premises of a known gangster. "So, what do you think?"

Staring at the photos, Herman expressed the same sentiments that Mike had. "There is no conflict here Mike. We have no active investigations involving Ki or his gang," pursing his lips in thought Herman continued. "If we did, you could simply recuse yourself from any part of the investigation."

Agreeing with Herman's synopsis, Mike added that most of Ki's criminal activities involve federal statutes.

Mike related to Herman that with the Feds knowing the family connection between himself and Ki, they were drooling at the thought of finally being able to insert a mole into Ki's operation.

"So, for the time being Herman I'm going to do nothing, I just wanted to apprise you of the situation in case those feds show up again."

Laughing out loud, Herman told Mike that based on what he had just witnessed in the squad room Mike needed no help.

Five days later, comfortably seated in a booth at Claude's Bistro, Mike had just finished the last bite of an incredibly delicious pastry stuffed with spicy meat. Now calmly sipping the remnants of Claude's spectacular house blend coffee, Mike was particularly vexed to see Federal Agent, Grant Armon approach his booth.

Watching with dis-interest as Armon slid into the booth and now sitting opposite him, a sarcastic Mike invited him to sit down.

"Why Thank-you Mike, I think I will," answered an equally sarcastic Grant.

SOLITARY TREE

"I apologize for that moron Stefanaski's actions the other day," began Grant. "The guy is a royal pain the ass, I'm sure you have your share of idiots in the twelfth Precinct. But, that's not why I'm here, I have spent the last two days reading a file that's gone cold, it appeared that almost a year ago, two young girls were abducted, and as per the latest addendums to the file, they have yet to be located. Does this ring a bell Mike?"

Mike leaned towards Grant as far as the table separating them would allow, and speaking very softly warned him the ice beneath his feet was beginning to crack. "I'm not sure where you are going with this Grant, but if I were you I would be very cautious," hissed Mike clenching his hands into fists so tight, the tendons over his knuckles protruded from the taut skin.

Holding up his hands with his palms facing outward in mock surrender, Grant assured Mike that he just wanted to run a hypothesis past him. "If I had two girls abducted, and the case had gone cold, with absolutely no hint of where they might be, I would use every means at my disposal to locate them."

Surmising that Grant was simply throwing Chum in the water in the hopes that something might bite, Mike maintained a stony-faced countenance as he replied. "If the agency you worked for had any abilities at all, my two girls would be sitting right here beside me, not you and your ugly face!" spat Mike derisively.

"Hey, I'm not the bad guy here Mike," rebutted a sympathetic Grant. "I told you I would use any means possible to find my girls, and I meant it. Try to hear what I'm saying," insisted Grant. "I don't blame you for using whatever means possible to locate your girls. This is one of those rare occasions where finding your girls, transcends crossing some lines. That's all I should say on that subject, other than I wish you all the luck in the world. I would also like to say that I was wrong the other day suggesting that you become our inside guy with Ki.

SOLITARY TREE

It was a knee jerk reaction to your disclosure of being related to Ki but, rest assured there are others in the agency that may not share my sentiments, and will pursue that end. Let's face it Mike, Stefananski is not your friend, and unfortunately his style of intimidation is admired at the Agency."

Surprised, yet at the same time somewhat skeptical of the tack taken by Grant, Mike surmised that he must for the time being accept it at face value.

Rising from the comfortable seat in the booth, Grant extended a hand that Mike shook, albeit reluctantly.

May tenth, the day that Mike had been dreading arrived, it's now been a full calendar year since he had seen his daughters. As the weeks and months inexorably pass by with no news of his girls, Mike slowly loses confidence in his ability to locate them. When he had approached Frankie the private investigator, he had thought that through her proven skills gleaning information from the internet, she might find something, but this has so far been fruitless. "It's like they fell into a black hole Mike," professed an extremely frustrated, and discouraged Frankie.

Deciding that he was not fit company for dinner with his landlords tonight, Mike hopped into his car and drove aimlessly around the city. As daylight slowly surrendered to the early evening twilight, the bright signs of Restaurants and Taverns heralding great food and drink chased away the shadows of night. Finding himself headed towards the suburbs where he now calls home, Mike observed the familiar sign of a neighborhood tavern. Walking into the subdued lighting of the main room, Mike took a moment to get his bearings. There were a couple of dozen people scattered between the booths that ran down one side of the room, the main area between himself and the bar was home to several randomly placed tables, there was even a miniscule dance floor to his immediate left. Situated at the bar were a dozen or so stools reserved for the serious drinkers, only half of which were currently occupied by people searching for answers, where no answers would be found.

SOLITARY TREE

Craving the solitude afforded by a booth, Mike made the short trek in search of an un-occupied booth. Glancing in the direction of the bored looking bartender, Mike motioned for two cold beers. Mike had barely sat down on the torn and abraded bench seat cushion, when a waitress placed two cardboard coasters on the rough plank table top, then with a flourish placed an ice cold looking bottle of beer on each coaster.
"Want a menu? "growled his waitress with the roughened voice of a cigarette smoker.
Looking at the name tag that identified his waitress as Gladice, he informed the hard-looking lady of fifty plus years, that a menu would indeed be very helpful.
"Be right back," she stated with a smile, that was as false as her ill-fitting dentures.
Taking a long, slow drink from one of the ice-cold bottles of beer, Mike relished the sharp clean taste as the beverage slid down his throat. Placing the bottle beside its twin, Mike watched the tear shaped drops of condensation race each other to the precipice waiting at the bottom of the bottle.
Flipping the menu on to the table Gladice asked Mike if he's ready to order. Smiling up at the hard looking Gladice, Mike informed her that he would like to look at the menu before deciding. But having said that since it's clear that Gladice has had a long hard shift Mike would spare her the walk back and place his order at the counter. Staring at Mike to see if he appreciated the fact that she had been on her feet for twelve hours, or if he is just being another smartass customer, Gladice soon gave up and with a short unpleasant sounding grunt headed off to another bothersome customer.
Enjoying another slow sip of his cold beverage, Mike figured since he had requested a menu from the hard bitten Gladice, the least he could do was look at it. The first item Mike saw on the single page; heavily stained menu was a clubhouse sandwich. Not caring what he ate, he figured he might as well go with the

clubhouse, true to his word he sauntered up to the counter and informed Gladice that he would like the clubhouse sandwich.
 Following a brief wait of ten minutes or so, Gladice deposited what Mike thought to be his clubhouse sandwich in front of him with a curt order to enjoy. Eyeing the sodden looking mass in front of him, Mike used the small fork provided with the meal to poke at it. Observing small gelatinous beads of fat emerge, Mike pushed the plate with the offensive sandwich to the far side of the table in disgust.
"Mike is that you?"
 Looking up, Mike was pleasantly surprised to see the petite figure of Mel Webster, who's employed as a Forensic Pathologist with the Medical Examiner's office.
 She has earned the respect of State prosecutors, as well as many defense attorneys, being completely unflappable when called upon to recite her findings in court. Despite many brow beatings from defense attorneys attempting to cast doubt upon her conclusions, she remained steadfast in her conviction that science does not lie. She's ferocious in her pursuit of the truth her motto is. "Only the facts please, I do not deal in hypothesis." Rising from his seat Mike shook Mel's tiny hand in greeting, as they exchanged pleasantries.
 "Are you having supper by yourself Mike?" Mel asked with curiosity etched across her pixie like features.
 Although still feeling the remnants of a lingering masochistic need to wallow in self-pity, and nurse his grief in solitude, Mike instinctively knew that Mel Webster would be better for him than any amount of alcohol. "As a matter of fact, I was Mel, but the clubhouse I ordered, is what sends people to their heart surgeons, so I was just drinking instead," finished Mike with boyish grin. "Are you meeting someone?" Mike asked tentatively.
"I was supposed to meet my dead-beat boyfriend here. I've explained to him that I was not going to live my life per his whims. It appears now that his standing me up like this is his immature way of saying that he quit, before he was fired."

Pointing to the booth, Mike advised her that she was more than welcome to join him for a drink if she so desired.

Staring up at Mike displaying an impish smile, Mel quickly agreed to join him.

Enquiring as to what she would like to drink, Mike grabbed the offensive club house and placed it on the countertop of the bar, advising the bored looking bartender that it wasn't fit for human consumption.

Returning in short order he made a show of first planting a coaster on the table directly in front of Mel, then placed the vodka martini onto the waiting coaster. Sliding into the booth opposite Mel, Mike was rewarded with a warm smile of gratitude.

"I do believe they have waitresses here that do that for you," bantered Mel.

Chuckling out loud Mike informed Mel that he and his waitress Gladice have reached an understanding, she will still receive a tip from Mike, but Mike must do all the legwork.

Laughing softly at this explanation, Mel raised her drink in a toast to new beginnings, softly touching her martini glass with his cold bottle of beer Mike seconds the toast.

The rest of the evening sped by, they enjoyed conversing about their respective workplaces, and the ever-present politics within.

Upon hearing that Mike was now Chief of Detectives at the twelfth precinct Mel congratulated him, then asked him if he colored his hair.

Laughing at this comment, Mike asked her why she thought he colored his hair.

"Well everyone knows that to be Chief of Detectives you have to be at least fifty years old, and have a beer belly," laughing out loud as she pointed to Mikes beer. "While constantly eating ant-acid tablets," concluded Mel with a pretty smile that showed off her pearly white teeth. "So, why is the new Chief of Detectives having a rather poor excuse for a supper, all by himself in this somewhat questionable establishment?" asked an inquisitive Mel.

SOLITARY TREE

Enjoying this brief interlude from the depressing thoughts that a year had passed, Mike was reluctant to alter the lighthearted tone of conversation they're enjoying, but decided that her question deserved an answer.

Finding an avid listener in Mel, it took Mike forty-five minutes to divulge all that had occurred over the last year, concluding with the fact that today marked one year since he had seen his daughters.

Mel, and Mike enjoyed a shared moment of laughter when he recalled his visit to the fortune teller, and the resulting information, that was forthcoming from that moment of irrationality.

Mel shook her head in dis-belief, when Mike relayed the fact that his now ex-wife showed no interest in searching for the girls.

Gazing sympathetically across the booth at Mike, she placed her hand on top of his and expressed her sincere belief that one day he will find his girls.

Glancing at her watch and seeing that two hours have sped by, she regrettably informed Mike that she had an early call in the morning, so she had better call it a night. Catching Gladice's eye Mike paid the bill and left a generous a ten-dollar tip, escorting Mel to the parking lot they assured each other that they were fine to drive.

Looking thoughtfully at Mike, Mel communicated to him that she would like to do this again. Mike was quick to second that idea, informing Mel that it's been a long time since he had felt this good. Promising to stay in touch, they exchanged a quick hug, with Mel brushing her lips lightly on Mike's left cheek as he bent down.

The next six weeks passed by uneventfully, Mike fully realizing that hiring Yolanda as his secretary was the smartest move he could have made. Her office management skills, combined with an effervescent personality made going to work each day almost enjoyable.

SOLITARY TREE

Mike has taken her several times to Claude's Bistro for lunch, introducing her to the incredibly talented French Canadian Chef. It was delightful watching the massively built chef inter-act with Yolanda, with the two of them forming an instant rapport.

On a sweltering summer night, laying on his bed wearing only boxers Mike glanced at his watch, bemoaning the fact it's midnight, and the humidity must be equal to the relentless heat. Tired of tossing and turning he arose from the bed, donning a pair of shorts used the private entryway to his suite, and sat outside where the light breeze at least dried the beads of sweat on his torso. After thirty minutes Mike felt the temperature begin to marginally fall, and decided that he might try sleeping again, when he heard a slight commotion from the main part of the house.

Hearing a loud cry of despair, Mike hurried back into his suite and using the basement suite stairway, ascended to the main floor of the home.

Opening the door that's never locked, Mike quietly called for Janine, hearing a low moaning sound he padded quietly on his bare feet tracking the sound to his landlord's bedroom.

Knocking softly on the door to gain her attention, Janine looked at Mike and with eyes red and inflamed from crying, informed Mike that she's afraid Fred had left them. Swearing softly, Mike moved quickly to the bedside and placed his first two fingers on Fred's throat desperately searching for a pulse.

It was when he touched Fred's skin that Mike realized he had been deceased for a while, despite the protracted heat of the night, Fred's skin was already cool to the touch. Looking over at Janine, Mike slowly shook his head in the negative, covering her face with her hands Janine released a long heart wrenching sob.

After the coroner's wagon, had left with Fred, Mike and Janine talked long into the night. Janine confided in Mike, that Fred and she were sadly, never able to conceive a child, they had considered adoption but for some reason it never came to fruition.

SOLITARY TREE

 She informed Mike, that she has a sister on the East Coast that she might go live with once she has sold the house. When Mike asked her about a service for Fred, she shook her head stating that most of their friends have either already passed away, or moved to another part of the country. "Fred always said he wanted to be cremated, and his urn put to sea allowing him to follow the ocean's currents," murmured the grief-stricken Janine.

 The week following the sudden death of Fred, was traumatic for both Janine and Mike, who had become very fond of his landlords. The first Monday following Fred's demise, Mike loaded up the wheel chair and followed the routine that himself and Fred, had been doing every Monday night the last few months of his life.

 Arriving at Jefferson High School Mike pushed the empty wheel chair into the gymnasium, and placed it exactly where Fred used to sit and applaud the Basketball players. As word of his death spread amongst the players, Mike was moved almost to the point of tears when the players one by one walked past the chair, nodding their heads at it, as though Fred was still occupying the chair.

 Seated at his desk Mike was considering his options, now that he might once again have to find new lodgings with Janine expressing the need to sell her home. Aimlessly drawing inter-connected circles on a pad of paper, the germ of an idea occurred to Mike. Rising from his chair he hurtled past a surprised Yolanda calling over his shoulder that he would be gone for a while. Like a man on a mission, Mike made his way to his car, only to stop suddenly when he spotted the immaculately dressed Scarface leaning up against the car's left rear fender.

 "Get your fuckin ass off my car!" demanded Mike.

 "Ki wants to see you," stated Scarface laconically.

 With a look of utter amazement Mike informed him that he was not Ki's lackey, and nor would he ever become one.

SOLITARY TREE

 Shrugging his massive shoulders in resignation at Mike's response, he simply warned Mike that when Ki wanted to see someone they better show up.

"You tell him for me, that I am not about to drop everything just because he requests an audience," avowed a defiant Mike.

 "I don't care what you do," stated the unruffled twin. "Ki asked me to contact you and I did. If you feel brave enough, or foolish enough to ignore the message then it's your funeral I guess." Having delivered his message, the twin moved to the car parked beside Mike's, then with a last, long look at Mike, got in and left.

 Still fuming at Ki's nerve, but knowing that since it was himself that initiated contact with Ki, he had better get used to the idea of seeing the twins show up unexpectedly.

 Arriving at Fred and Janine's house Mike parked his car and entered his basement suite through his private entryway, ascending the stairs to the main part of the house, Mike knocked politely on the door before entering the kitchen.

"Oh Mike!" exclaimed a surprised Janine, replacing the black phone onto its cradle. "I was just about to call you. Why don't you sit down at the table, there's some things I would like to discuss with you?"

 Seating himself in one of the four wooden chairs at the mid-sized rounded kitchen table, Mike prepared himself to hear Janine explain to him that he must move out.

 Sitting down opposite Mike, Janine began speaking. "I have been doing some serious thinking Mike, and I have a proposal I would like to share with you. Since Fred and myself never had any children, there is no one to leave our house to. My needs are not great since I will be living with my sister, so I would like to know if you would care to buy our home."

 Smiling at Janine, a pleased looking Mike explained to her that the reason he came home early was to run that very idea by her. He went on to say that this is the type of home he had always hoped to share with his wife and daughters.

SOLITARY TREE

Writing something down on her kitchen recipe notepad, Janine tore the page off and offered it to Mike. Viewing what was written on the paper, Mike realized that the number written on the paper represented what Janine would like for the house.

"Janine!" protested Mike. "This figure is less than half of what you could get for this house."

Smiling at Mike as though he were her son, she reiterated the fact that her needs were not great, and knowing that Mike would take good care of the home, that she and Fred shared for so many years was worth more than any amount of money.

Two days later, Mike made arrangements with a charter boat captain to transport them out to sea, where he assured Mike an ocean current would grant Fred his wish.

A scorching morning sun, with an azure colored sky heralded the day that Fred was going to begin his final journey. Janine and Mike drove sixty miles to the West Port Marina where they met Captain Mark Weaver, and his boat The Flying Dolphin. The Flying Dolphin measured twenty -six feet from stem to stern, and possessed a beam of ten feet. The twin one hundred horsepower outboard motors, soon had them skipping across the top of a light chop. In no time at all they arrived at their destination twenty miles from shore, this is where their Captain assured them that Fred's urn would catch an outgoing current.

Giving Janine her privacy for this final farewell, Mike and the Captain discreetly retired to the covered bridge. Fifteen minutes later a badly shaken Janine appeared, and asked Mike if they could return to shore. Mike quickly put his arm around the trembling shoulders of Janine, at the same time asked Mark if he had a blanket. Producing a thick wool blanket, he passed it to Mike, who wrapped the weighty, rough textured blanket around Janine. Helping her to sit down, Mike sat beside her putting his arm around her, offering both his comfort and his strength during this extremely difficult time.

When they arrived back at the marina Mike thanked the Captain, and pointing at the blanket was told to keep it.

SOLITARY TREE

 Assisting the catatonic, and very weak Janine back to the car, and despite the sweltering temperature outside, Mike turned the heat on in the car. They were almost halfway home before Janine shrugged off the blanket and reached over to turn the heat off, looking closely at Mike and seeing beads of sweat running freely off his brow she whispered. "You're such a dear Mike; you will make some lucky lady very happy."

 Two days later Mike sadly bestowed a good-bye hug upon Janine, as she boarded a plane headed East, and a future without the partner she had shared her life with.

CHAPTER EIGHT

Proudly sitting outside on the front steps of his newly acquired four-bedroom home on a hot Sunday afternoon, Mike had taken a short break from mowing his lawn. Wiping the sweat off his brow, he had earlier removed his soaking wet Tee shirt much to the delight of the lady next door. Gazing at his lawn that was slowly losing its battle with the summer time heat, and turning golden brown in places, Mike wondered idly if this will be as good as his life gets.

Watching his phone begin to vibrate its way across his front porch, Mike reached over and answered it.

"Nephew!" barked the unmistakable voice of Ki. "When I order someone to see me, I expect that person to show up."

"Well you better get used to the fact Ki, that I refuse to jump at your beck and call. I'm not one your paid lackeys, if you think that I am, then you're sorely mistaken," growled Mike into the phone.

"What happened to that phone I gave you?" demanded Ki. "You really need to check it occasionally nephew."

Mike was about to tell Ki that he could go to hell, when he heard the tell-tale click of Ki hanging up.

Muttering out loud that. "Ki could go fuck himself," Mike carried on with the serious business of cutting his lawn. Later that same day moving through his kitchen, Mike stopped and stared at the familiar table with its four chairs. Wanting to save Janine the trouble and heartache of having to sell her furniture, Mike had paid her more than she requested for the house and retained the furniture.

SOLITARY TREE

Opening the counter drawer that housed the eating utensils, Mike removed two knives, two forks, and two spoons, carrying the utensils to the table he carefully, and lovingly set two places.

Removing two drinking glasses from the cupboard, as well as two dinner plates he completed the task of setting two places where hopefully one day he would see his daughters sitting.

That evening he remembered the call from Ki, walking the short distance to his car he retrieved the phone from its resting place in the vehicle's consul. Opening a cold beer from the refrigerator, Mike sat down at the kitchen table and placed the phone on the smooth table top. Staring at the phone, Mike was leery of what could be on it that is important enough to have Ki call him. Following the phone's prompts to input his personal code, Mike was horror-struck at what the phone contained.

There's an extremely clear image of two men holding a third hapless victim upside down over a railing, that is at least twenty-five feet above the ground. The voices of the three people are incredibly clear, the one being held up-side down is pleading for his life, while the two holding him by his ankles are laughing at him. Then to Mike's horror the one guy shouted that he's losing his grip, then as if in slow motion it looked like they simply let go, the person recording this horrific event than focused on the faces of the two men, and Mike instantly recognized the faces of Detective Hans Albright, and Detective Greg Spence. The video ended abruptly, when it began playing again it clearly showed Albright and Spence placing the blanket wrapped body in what appeared to be the trunk of an abandoned vehicle. As the short video clip came to an end, there followed the words that Mike should call Ki.

"I take it you have watched the video," remarked Ki for-going any form of greeting.

SOLITARY TREE

"This is apparently the way your upstanding detectives mete out justice. This video was shot by a neighbor who thought that I might be interested in purchasing this footage. He was right, I sent that copy to your phone, but I still retain a copy.

You have exactly seventy -two hours from now to act on it, if I feel that your actions regarding this footage are not conclusive enough then it goes public."

"Why send it to me?" asked Mike.

"Think about it nephew, who better to get rid of two cops then another cop. Just think of the amusement I will have watching the evening news, as they report how a good Samaritan videotaped two cops killing an innocent person. It will be so pleasurable watching you inform the viewing public the reason why the Detectives were being fired."

"What if I refuse to play your little game!" demanded an incensed Mike.

"Dearest nephew have you already forgotten that I have the original copy." Then in a voice that harbored no warmth whatsoever, Ki informed Mike that if the seventy-two hours elapsed without a news conference by the Police Department, regarding the actions of the two Detectives, it would be turned over to the media. They would also be advised that Chief of Detectives, Michael Chance was in possession of the tape and refused to take appropriate action.

"That would ruin my career," stated Mike with growing apprehension

"Yes, dear nephew I'm afraid your career as a cop would be over, but you could always come to work for me," chuckled Ki.

"Fuck you Ki," hissed Mike vehemently.

"Now Mike really, is that any way for you to talk to your uncle. Before you get mad and hang up, you will need a body for your impotent legal system, the deceased gentleman's name is Allen Wong, he made a career of being a low-level drug dealer who always dreamed of being the number one dealer in town.

SOLITARY TREE

He was becoming a thorn in my side so it's no great loss," Ki reported nonchalantly, as if he were simply discussing the weather. "Anyways under the railway bridge off First street there are several abandoned vehicles, you will find what you seek in the trunk of the blue car on the left. Of course, in this heat, I'm sure your nose will direct you to it."

About to verbally harangue Ki, Mike realized Ki had hung up.

"Sonofabitch," hollered Mike, barely able to restrain himself from placing the phone under his heel, and grinding it into miniscule pieces of glass and plastic. Giving in to that impulse would certainly be the end of Mike's career, as he instinctively knew that Ki would derive great pleasure in seeing three cops go down instead of two. Mike had known that becoming involved with Ki was tantamount to pulling the tail of a Tiger, and that he may very well get bitten, unfortunately for Mike he felt he had no recourse if he wanted help in finding his girls. Ki's criminal network reached far and wide, this provided him entry into a world that Mike only had nightmares about. What's pissed Mike off, is the fact that Ki now thinks he can dictate to Mike how he will think and act.

Glancing at his watch he noted it was just slightly past seven pm, deciding to go for a drive he headed towards the railway bridge that Ki had described. After a quick thirty-minute drive through light Sunday evening traffic, Mike turned off First Street and drove down the gently sloped hill to the large flat area under the Railway crossing, immediately spotting the cars that Ki had described parked haphazardly in the tall brown grass.

Mike brought his vehicle to a halt, reluctantly exiting his vehicle he was instantaneously assaulted by the stench of putrefying flesh. "Jesus Christ," muttered Mike breathing through his mouth attempting to by-pass his offended olfactory sense.

Wondering how nobody had noticed the cloying stench and reported it, Mike hopped back into his car and its relative stench free environment. Drumming the fingers of his right hand against the car's steering wheel, Mike pondered his next move.

SOLITARY TREE

With the clock voraciously devouring the seventy-two hours that Ki imposed, Mike recognized the fact that time was of the essence. The unfortunate part of this scenario was, its Sunday evening, and Mike would lose the next ten hours before he could meet with anyone about this.

Entering his office at six-thirty Monday morning after a sleepless night, Mike once again reviewed his strategy.

Having checked the work schedule that Yolanda had posted last Friday afternoon, he was cognizant of the fact that Detective Hans Albright, and his partner Greg Spence were scheduled to work the eight am to four pm shift. Hearing voices in the squad room Mike moved to his office door to see who was in the squad room, not surprised he watched Albright unsuccessfully attempt to ingratiate himself with Yolanda. Smiling warmly at Yolanda as she placed her purse and brown lunch bag on her desk, before going to make her tea, Mike bid her good morning. Glancing at Mike she thanked him, then observing his body language asked him what's going on. "You firing me this morning boss?" she enquired with a coquettish smile.

Staring at Albright, Mike quietly assured Yolanda that he would be lost without her invaluable help. Noticing that Greg Spence had also arrived in the squad room, Mike bellowed out to Albright and Spence that he needed to see them in his office right fucking now. Stunned into silence by the ferocity evident in Mike's voice, the remaining Detectives in the room quickly found somewhere else to be. As the two detectives nonchalantly made their way towards Mike's office, they were still bantering about who drank whom under the table Friday night.

Closing the office door in firmly, Mike pointed to the chairs and ordered the two to sit.

"What's up Mike?" chirped Albright, with an annoying smirk. adding that it looked like Mike had his tail in a knot about something.

"Shut the fuck up Albright!" growled Mike.

"Hey no need to get rude!" objected Spence.

SOLITARY TREE

Pointing a large index finger at Spence, Mike also warned him to shut up. Picking up the phone lying in the middle of his desk, Mike navigated through the personal identification process, then placed it back down in front of the two Detectives and started the video. Glowering at the two as the video played, Mike watched them quickly glance at each other in horror.

"Where in the fuck did you get this?" demanded Albright.

"Doesn't really matter does it," responded Mike.

"It's a fake. Someone is trying to frame us!" thundered Albright.

"Nothing to say Spence?" growled Mike. "Okay assholes, guns and badges on the desk."

"Fuck you Chance! Like fuck you're getting my gun and my badge," declared Spence breaking his silence.

"You have exactly ten seconds to place your guns and badges on my desk, I guarantee you that you will not like the consequences if you fail to do so," threatened Mike quietly.

Looking as though he were about to continue to protest, Spence broke first and with a quietly muttered expletive placed his weapon and badge on the desk. Cursing out loud a defiant Albright soon followed suit and deposited his weapon and badge on the desk alongside those of Spence.

Picking up the items Mike moved to his office door, opening the door he motioned for Detective Herman Diaz to approach. When Diaz entered the office, Mike informed him to arrest both Albright and Spence on suspicion of murder, completely mystified with what had occurred Diaz complied with Mike's order and placed the two under arrest.

"Handcuffs to!" barked Mike. "Behind their backs not in front, read them their rights, then take them to booking and process them."

As the trio left the office Mike sank into his chair, leaned forward placing his elbows on the desktop closed his eyes and rested his forehead in his open palms.

SOLITARY TREE

Knowing that Spence and Albright had committed murder, then attempted to cover it up did nothing to erase the bad taste in Mike's mouth as he wondered if he was now Ki's puppet.

"Are you alright Mike," Yolanda asked quietly from the just inside the office door.

Not lifting his head, Mike muttered through his palms that he was not sure if he will ever be alright.

With the clock still ticking, Mike lifted his head, picked up his desk phone and placed a call to the District Attorney's office. After introducing himself he asked the receptionist if he could speak with Al Coltrane, she informed him that Al was tied up in meetings until at least noon. With time slipping away, a desperate Mike asked if there was an assistant District Attorney he could meet with. While waiting for her to check schedules, Mike mentally tallied the hours left to him, and what he needed to have transpire with- in that time frame.

An impatient Mike was finally advised that he could meet with Rachel, she was an assistant District Attorney and could be in your office in an hour.

Thanking her, Mike replaced the phone in its cradle. A very business-like Rachel arrived at Mike's office thirty-five minutes later. Glancing at her as she entered his office, Mike observed a lady of perhaps thirty years old with an athletic looking body, short brunette hair, blue eyes and tastefully applied make-up.

After introducing himself, Mike immediately launched into the details of the case against Detectives Albright and Spence. While viewing the video, Rachel began scribbling notes on her pad of white, legal sized lined paper.

As the short video came to an end, Rachel's first question to Mike was. "How did you happen to come into possession of this video Mike?"

"I feel that how I obtained the video is immaterial. What I need to know is, based on the video do you have enough to formally charge Albright and Spence with murder?" asked Mike.

"How I obtained the video will be argued about in court, if it even gets that far," asked Mike.

With pursed lips Rachel studied her scribbled notes, unconsciously tapping her pencil softly against her chin, that was channeled by a slight cleft. After carefully weighing the video and her notes for a full minute, Rachel nodded her head in the affirmative. "I will run this by Al, he will have the final say," cautioned Rachel. "This will be a highly inflammatory case, two cops dropping a guy on his head will be front page news. I'm sure Al will want to prosecute this case himself. Right now, though I will proceed with charges of Murder in the Second Degree, of course Al will have the final word on how we proceed, if we even proceed with charges. I will bring this matter to his attention as soon as possible." Pointing at the phone Rachel enquired if Mike had an envelope that it could be placed into, she then informed him that this case will not be good for an already much maligned Police Department, and she cautioned Mike, that the political will to pursue charges against these two Detectives may not be present.

"With all due respect, Rachel, I strongly dis-agree. This will demonstrate to the public that we are able to police ourselves, and if warranted be prosecuted the same as anyone else," Mike rebutted forcefully.

Leaving the office, Rachel informed Mike that she would be in touch.

Mike's next call was to the Medical Examiner's office, giving the receptionist the location of the deceased, being very circumspect in not revealing the fact that he already knew the deceased's name, he requested a team be dispatched there for cadaver retrieval. Hanging up the phone, Mike noticed Herman standing just outside his office door. "Those two assholes get processed?" enquired Mike.

"Yep they're being processed as we speak," confirmed Diaz.

"Okay, let's go for a ride," stated Mike.

SOLITARY TREE

As they drove to the site of the deceased, Mike brought Herman up to speed on the details of the case, omitting any inkling as to how he came to possess the video.

Arriving at the site Mike was surprised to see the Medical Examiner's van already there, he had not expected to see them there for at least an hour.

Exiting their vehicle Mike was again assaulted by the nauseating stench of decaying flesh, with Diaz also choking on the pervading stench, he glanced over at Mike and with a mirthless smile stated. "You must be still pissed about that interview, that's why you brought me here to enjoy this."

Shaking his head in denial Mike assured Diaz that this was not the case, locating a vantage point that was upwind from the stench, Mike and Diaz watch the pair of Forensic Pathologists perform their grisly task of cadaver retrieval. With paper cover-all's, and hazardous material breathing apparatus on, they carried out their task with an air of professional detachment.

After a period of approximately thirty minutes in which time they spent photographing the entire scene and collecting samples, they finally removed the deceased from the trunk and placed him on a gurney. After re-loading the now corpse laden gurney into their van, one of the two team members headed towards where Mike and Diaz were patiently waiting.

Nodding his head at Mike and Diaz, he introduced himself as Blair Underwood, then with a smile apologized stating. "For obvious reasons, I won't shake hands."

Agreeing quickly, Mike assured him that they were not offended in the least, then introduced himself and Diaz.

As Blair blew a small air bubble with the gum he was chewing, Mike chuckled and apprised Blair that he knew Mel Webster and that she also chewed gum.

"We all do," Blair replied. "Sometimes it helps with the smell." Advising Mike that they were done here, he turned and headed back to the van.

SOLITARY TREE

Returning to his office Mike glanced at his watch, and grimaced when he realized it's already two p.m., and no word from the D. A's office.

At the sound of someone knocking on his door Mike looked up from a report he was reading, and observed the Police Captains personal hatchet man Lieutenant William Bowers, lounging in the doorway.

"Captain wants to see you," ordered Bowers.

Even though Mike was sure what the Captain wanted to see him about, he still felt compelled to ask Bowers why.

Shrugging his shoulders. "I don't know, and I don't care," answered Bowers bluntly, the look in his eyes though gave lie to his words. He knew exactly why the Captain wanted to see him. "The Captain asked me to come get you, so here I am. Let's go," he ordered.

Walking into the Captain's spacious, though Spartan like waiting room, the receptionist behind the large desk waved them in the direction of the Captain's office advising them the Captain was expecting them.

Entering the inner office with its similarly Spartan like furnishings, Mike was greeted frostily by the Captain. Nodding his head in the direction of two straight backed wooden chairs Mike was invited to sit. It was only then that Mike noticed Al Coltrane the District Attorney himself, sitting quietly at a small desk against the far wall.

"Thanks Bill, that will be all," the Captain stated, dismissing Bowers from the room.

"Well Mike, it would appear that we have a royal clusterfuck," began the captain coldly. "You do realize that what you have done is unprecedented, never in the entire history of this Police Department has the Chief of Detectives charged two of his own detectives with murder!"

As the Captain stared coldly at him, Mike was once again reminded of stories told by others about how ferocious the Captain used to be when he was a street cop.

SOLITARY TREE

"I have seen the video that came into your possession, at this point in time Al, and myself agree that how you came to possess it, is academic. I am quite frankly pissed however, that you saw fit to proceed with arresting and charging those two miscreants without first informing me. You must know that the charge sheet is open to the media, we need to carefully orchestrate this incident so that it does not bite us in the ass."

At this juncture, the Captain motioned for Al to join them. "Al and myself have thought this through and this is how we will proceed. Albright and Spence have been formally charged, but none of today's actions will be made public until a news conference is held at three pm, Wednesday. To that end we have buried the record of arrest and charges against those two assholes."

Seated on the hard, uncomfortable wooden chair Mike quickly calculated the time frame with respect to Ki's imposed deadline, feeling a sense of relief wash over him realizing that if everything proceeded as the Captain stated, then he should have a couple of hours to spare.

The Captain interrupted Mike's calculations as he continued in the same cold voice. "As I stated earlier, I am pissed that you proceeded without first informing me, but at the same time I admire you for knowing what needed to be done then doing it. I have devoted too much of my life to this Police Department to let two assholes undo what I'm trying to achieve. We have to earn the public's trust, and to do so Albright and Spence will feel the full brunt of the law, the same that any other person would."

Rising from his chair he extended his right hand towards Mike, who quickly rose from the uncomfortable wooden chair and shook the Captains proffered hand.

"I knew I had chosen the right man for the job, this was a tough decision Mike, and you never flinched from your sense of duty!" commended the Captain.

SOLITARY TREE

"With all due respect sir," began Mike. "It was a relatively easy decision, there's irrefutable evidence contained in the video that, Spence and Albright committed murder, then took pains to cover it up."

"Mike, I have been in this Police Department for many years, mayhap too many years," the Captain mused, then continued. "I have heard of many events concerning all levels of the Police Department being buried that should have been made public. There were times that perhaps I could have spoken up, but chose not to, so, it gives me great pleasure realizing that you are the new breed of cop. You will always do what's best for the Department, you will not shirk your responsibility to the Department!" concluded the captain emphatically. It was at this point that he seemed to realize he still grasped Mike's hand and released it.

"Thank-you for your vote of confidence in my dedication to the Department Captain, I just hope I am able to meet your expectations."

After a few quick words with Al concerning the evidence against the detectives, Mike left the Captain's office. Feeling mildly guilty regarding his subterfuge, Mike assuaged this feeling knowing that he would have proceeded the same way with or without Ki's ultimatum.

Wednesday's news conference went off without a hitch. At exactly three pm., it was announced that Detectives Hans Albright, and Greg Spence had been relieved of their duties, and have been charged with second degree murder in the death of Mr. Allen Wong.

Exactly twenty minutes after the news conference concluded Mike felt his cell phone begin to vibrate in his pants pocket. Answering the call, he was not surprised to hear Ki's voice congratulate him on beating the deadline. Ki informed him that he had a reward for Mike, and that Mike should proceed to the address that will be sent in a text format to Mike's phone as soon as Ki hung up.

SOLITARY TREE

True to his word no sooner had Ki ended the call, when Mike received an address that was in a very rundown part of the city. Most cops that are unfortunate enough to get dispatched to that area, ensure they have back-up close by.

It took Mike forty-five minutes in the congested afternoon traffic to arrive at his destination, the outside of the building was to say the least forbidding. Where there were once windows, there was now plywood, the front yard looked like it had been the recipient of the neighborhood's garbage for the last five years. The two objects that looked completely foreign to this neighborhood, were two, shiny black, four door vehicles parked in the weed filled driveway. With mounting trepidation Mike carefully picked his way through the garbage strewn front yard, reaching what passed for a front door, Mike carefully examined it to ensure it would not fall onto him when he opened it.

He need not have worried as it was opened for him, by none other than Scarface, dressed as always in the tux. Nodding his head in a silent greeting, Scarface indicated to Mike that he should follow him. As Mike followed the massive figure through what looked to be at one time the kitchen of the dwelling, they soon reached a flight of stairs heading into a basement.

Descending into the poorly lit basement Mike's apprehension was rapidly increasing, to the point of wanting the reassurance of his weapon in his hand, not his holster. Mike was not surprised to find Ki waiting at the bottom of the staircase, holding his hand out Ki demanded to see Mike's phone. Somewhat cautiously Mike handed his phone to Ki, and watched as he expertly opened the back cover and removed the memory card, placing the memory card under his boot heel he methodically ground it into the cement. Smiling at Mike he informed him that he will need a new memory card, Ki then returned the phone to Mike along with another one. "The second phone is to replace the one that we no longer have access to," stated Ki quietly. "Now the little matter of the reward I mentioned to you earlier."

SOLITARY TREE

Ki spoke in what sounded to Mike like Cantonese to Scarface who quickly opened a heavy wooden door, moving with surprising agility for one so big, Scarface disappeared into the room with Ki and a vigilant Mike following.

The room they have entered surprised Mike by its size, it was at least fifteen feet wide by twenty feet long, there was one single light bulb burning in the center of the room, whose feeble halo of light did nothing to dispel the murky shadows. As Mike's vision began to adjust to the gloom, he realized that there were other people in the room, just outside the halo of light stood three other men. The one man who Mike recognized as Scarface's twin, in unison with a second man were clearly supporting the weight of a third person.

Looking at a third man standing in the shadow's, Ki demanded to know if the person being restrained had talked. Shaking his head in the negative, Ki threw up his hands up in the air in resignation.

Wondering what the fuck was going on Mike's hand began to move unobtrusively towards his gun, when his hand came to rest on the holster, he delicately slipped the thong off the gun's hammer that secured the weapon to the holster. As the two burly men brought their captive out of the shadows and into the halo of weak light, Mike instantly recognized the man that he had come to hate like no other. With a roar that emanated from his very soul, Mike attacked Gwyn O'Mallory the man that was the driving force behind the abduction of his girls. Throwing punches that landed like bombs on the body and head of O'Mallory, if not for the intervention of Scarface and his twin brother, O'Mallory would have died under the onslaught. The twins as big as they are, were barely able to restrain the raging Mike who was caught in the grips of a mindless fury.

Watching with a look of complete dis-interest as this scene was played out in front of him, Ki uttered a short phrase in Cantonese to the twins, nodding their heads in assent they continued to restrain Mike.

SOLITARY TREE

For Mike's benefit, Ki switched back to English and informed him that if continued to disrupt the proceedings, he had ordered the twins to shoot Mike.

Shaking off the clutching hands of the twins Mike took two large breaths, and continued to stare at O'Mallory while growling at Ki that he was in control.

Mike still couldn't believe it only took Ki a short time to locate and apprehend O'Mallory, the Feds as well as countless local police authorities had thus far been stymied in their efforts to locate him.

"You have ten minutes to ask him what you need to know," stated Ki abruptly.

Wasting no time Mike began firing a barrage of questions at the beaten, bleeding O'Mallory. "Where the fuck are my girls?" bellowed Mike.

"Don't know," muttered O'Mallory.

"What do you mean you don't know. You took them back from Jacobs in Peach City!"

"Ya, after that we didn't know what we were going to do with them. Thought maybe we were going to have to kill them, then Ellen met some guy who said he would buy them off us," murmured O'Mallory so quietly he was almost inaudible.

"Where's Ellen now?" barked Mike sharply.

"Dunno, after we sold the brats to that other guy, she left saying she never wanted to see me again."

With this revelation of what had befallen his girls, Mike's black eyes were burning holes through O'Mallory, the sheer unadulterated hatred he felt for this man knew no bounds.

"Where's Donovan?" asked Mike coldly.

"Looking for me I guess," muttered O'Mallory. "That asshole actually bragged about killing my nephews."

"Ya, I saw the Delveccio boys they weren't looking too good," confirmed Mike.

SOLITARY TREE

As Ki watched this by-play between Mike and O'Mallory he displayed little if any emotion, he finally intervened and informed them that the ten minutes were up.

"So, Mike, what are we to do? When you mentioned this gentleman's name I was quite surprised. To say that I located him just for you would be false, I had invested a considerable amount of time and resources seeking this wayward individual." Pointing in the direction of O'Mallory Ki went on to explain to Mike, that O'Mallory had earlier reached a business arrangement with Ki that he failed to live up to.

"I made an error in judgement when I loaned this good man a significant amount of money, with the understanding that he would repay me in short order. When you had informed me that O'Mallory was the force behind your daughter's abduction I then realized that he had no intention of repaying the good faith loan." Rubbing his chin thoughtfully Ki continued. "So, we have a bit of an awkward situation here, I'm positive about what you would like to see happen Mike, but if that happens then I will never recover my investment however, I'm sure that Mr. O'Mallory here was going to renege on his loan anyways, so nephew it looks like you may win and I may lose."

Not making any sudden moves, Mike slowly extracted his weapon form its holster, watching carefully and with a ghost of a smile, Ki once again barked out a short sequence of Cantonese.

Feeling a hand on his shoulder, Mike turned and was surprised when Scarface handed him a weapon that was equipped with a silencer.

"You do not want to use your own," he cautioned.

Accepting the proffered weapon, Mike slowly turned and calmly fired a bullet into the left knee of O'Mallory, with O'Mallory screaming in pain and only having one leg to support him, the two men holding him were hard pressed to keep him upright.

"Last chance, O'Mallory," declared Mike with deadly intent. "Where are my girls?"

"I don't know!" screamed O'Mallory. "You can't kill me, we're both cops, we're the blue wall," screamed O'Mallory.

SOLITARY TREE

Taking exaggerated aim, Mike fired a bullet into O'Mallory's remaining uninjured knee, with both legs now unable to lend any support at all, the two handlers simply allowed O'Mallory to fall to the cold cement floor and writhe in pain.
Smiling mirthlessly at his nephew, Ki informed him that he thought it quite ironic, when Mike told O'Mallory it's his last chance.
"So, what are you going to do now Mike?" asked Ki. "Maybe call the paramedics to come and rescue this guy."
Staring at his uncle, Mike walked the four short steps to where O'Mallory was curled up in a fetal position on the floor sobbing in pain, his hands gripping his bullet torn knees. Mike lifted his right foot and placed it on O'Mallory's shoulder and pressed down, forcing O'Mallory onto his back, staring up at Mike through a river of tears O'Mallory's pleas for mercy fell on deaf ears. Staring down at O'Mallory without a shred of remorse Mike coldly told him. "You took everything that I loved away from me, now I will take everything from you," whereupon the gun hiccupped four times in rapid succession, ending O'Mallory's allotted time on earth
"It would appear the cub has grown some teeth," remarked a thoughtful Ki.
Walking back to Scarface, Mike returned the weapon, and without another word left the darkness of the room, for the light at the top of the stairs.
Ascending the stairs from the gloomy basement that now reeked of death, Mike heard Ki telling him to stay in touch. With his head tilted slightly to the side tracking Mike's heavy tread as he vacated the premises, once Ki was convinced that Mike would not return he motioned to an almost invisible figure standing motionless in the darkest corner of the room. "Did you get it all?" questioned Ki

SOLITARY TREE

In answer to Ki's question a specter like figure, dressed in black, and wearing black grease paint on his face, dis-engaged himself from the shadows he had cloaked himself in, and passed a small video camera to Ki. A vicious smile played across the lips of Ki as he watched the video unfold. "That's perfect, well done Chang," stated Ki enthusiastically. "Your technical wizardry never ceases to amaze me." As the videographer, Chang made ready to leave the room, Ki informed him that Scarface's twin brother Edward had an envelope for him.

Upon hearing Ki say this, Edward quickly extracted a thick envelope from his jacket's inside pocket and tossed it to Chang.

"Take your family on a holiday," crowed a beaming Ki.

"Do you have that plastic bag I asked you to bring Edward?"

Passing a large plastic bag to his boss, Ki carefully placed the weapon Mike had used to kill O'Mallory, along with the video camera into the bag and secured the top.

"What do you want done with the dead guy?" asked Scarface.

With a look of disgust at the lifeless body of O'Mallory, Ki ordered them to burn the fucking house, with O'Mallory in it.

CHAPTER NINE

Staring at the calendar on his desk, Mike couldn't believe how fast the time had flown, it's been four months since the first anniversary of his daughter's abduction. He had settled comfortably into his new role as Chief of Detectives, to the point that the daily routine had become mundane. He's taken on a few cases of his own just to break up the monotony of his daily existence. It's been six weeks since the arrest of detectives Spence and Albright for murder, that case was now mired in the sluggish wheels of the justice system. There had been a report in the media of an abandoned house burning down, this had at first not captured Mike's attention, until it was announced that bone fragments had been discovered in the basement. Mike realized that this was Ki's method of destroying evidence, approached by the Fire Chief with this development, Mike had assigned one of his more phlegmatic detectives to investigate this discovery.

Last week, Mike had called Frankie, the private detective he had hired only to learn that she had suffered a heart attack and was recuperating at home. He had Yolanda send some flowers and a get-well card, smiling as he remembered how she had bristled at the idea of Mike sending another woman flowers, until he had explained who Frankie was and her age.

Looking up at the sound of a discreet knock, Mike found himself admiring the lithe, athletic form of Yolanda, attired in close-fitting tan colored slacks and peach hued short sleeved blouse, glide into his office, and perch lightly on the arm of a chair.

"We need to have a party!" she announced.

SOLITARY TREE

"We do?" questioned Mike. Smiling at this sudden declaration, Mike asked her under what pre-text do they need to have a party.

"You have had your house for three months now, it's high time you had a house warming party," asserted Yolanda.

Lightly teasing her, Mike informed Yolanda that his house was quite warm enough, thank-you.

"You know very well what I mean Mike," stated Yolanda feigning anger.

"Okay, you say I need to have a party to warm my house," contemplated Mike out loud. "What would happen if no one came to the party, just think how embarrassing that would be."

"You let me worry about that," avowed a cheerful Yolanda." Rising from the arm of the chair she moved around Mike's desk to better see his calendar and pick a date. With Yolanda standing so near, Mike could detect a subtle fragrance that suggested the scent one might encounter in an orchard full of peaches trees.

Having decided on a Saturday night two weeks hence, Mike informed her that since she wanted to have the party, it would be up to her to organize it.

"It will be my pleasure," pronounced the vivacious Yolanda with a warm smile. "Oh and by the way Mike, you might want to get a haircut, pretty soon your curls will be hiding your ears," suggested Yolanda with an amused wink.

Watching her leave the office, Mike was not exactly sure he wanted or needed a party, but as it appeared to be out of his hands, and since it will be at his home he must show up, and smile.

Leaving all the planning and invitations to the vibrant Yolanda, Mike made one call to invite someone whom he thought about quite often, only to be told that she was on an extended personal leave and couldn't be reached. A disappointed Mike decided to leave his address and the date for the party with the receptionist, in the hopes that she might show up.

SOLITARY TREE

A bubbly Yolanda dressed in form fitting jeans, and light sweater arrived at Mike's house at noon on the day of the festivities, as Mike gave her a brief tour of his home, Yolanda noticed the two places set at the kitchen table and apologized for being early, thinking Mike was expecting someone for lunch.

As Mike explained to her the significance of the two place settings, Yolanda listened with a thoughtful expression. Overcome by emotion as Mike quietly expressed his fervent wish that one day his daughters would be seated at this table with him, Yolanda moved close to Mike and hugged him tightly. Somewhat disconcerted by this personal touch, Mike advised Yolanda that he was off to a barber to get his curls reined in, and that she would have the house to herself for a couple of hours to prepare for the party.

True to his word Mike arrived back home in a couple of hours with closely cropped curls. He was amazed at the transformation that had occurred in his house, there were strategically placed balloons and streamers, an impromptu bar was now situated on his kitchen counter. There was a note placed on his kitchen table from Yolanda, advising Mike the caterer will arrive at six pm, and that she will return shortly after six pm as well. This left Mike wondering how much this party that he didn't want in the first place, was going to cost him.

After a scalding hot shower, Mike dressed in dark slacks and a light pull over sweater, was relaxing on his back deck enjoying a cold beer when he heard the front door chimes. Cursing silently, he headed to the front door to see who was brave enough to interrupt his quiet time, opening the door Mike was surprised when he saw none other than Claude, the owner of Claude's Bistro standing on his front porch.

As the massive French, Canadian bulled his way past Mike, he began bellowing orders to what looked like a small army of assistants.

SOLITARY TREE

Watching as they took over his home, Mike admired their handiwork as they quickly laid out a marvelous looking buffet. In no time at all they had pre-cooked Shrimp, joined by Prawns resting side by side on an ice-covered platter with a smattering of green leafy vegetables.

There were countless varieties of cold meats and of course, some of Claude's own specialties. It took less than twenty minutes for Claude and his assistants to work their magic, as Claude was shaking his hand and taking his leave, Yolanda arrived.

Mike was mesmerized by her appearance, dressed in a powder blue dress, with a like colored scarf, and wearing a light sweater against the chill of a late September evening, she was the epitome of radiance as she exited her car and walked towards Mike. Even Claude emitted along low whistle of appreciation, which caused Yolanda to blush slightly. Stopping in front of Mike, she performed a slow twirl, at the same time asking him if he thought her dress would be alright. A slightly tongue tied Mike informed her that she looked perfect.

"You look perfect yourself Mike, your hair looks very nice," she added with a radiant smile.

As parties go, Mike thought Yolanda had out done herself, it seemed that she had invited a cross section of people from every division of the Police Department. With Yolanda acting as hostess, Mike could finally slip away, and sit in the relative quiet, and comfortable solitude of his front porch. Sipping on a cold beer, enjoying this moment of tranquility, Mike allowed his mind to briefly imagine that was his wife Adele, inside being the captivating hostess, with Alicia and Desiree sleeping in their beds. Hearing a car door close, Mike was jerked back to reality, looking curiously at the car Mike wondered who the latecomer was. As the click of shoe heels on the cement driveway approached through the shadowy darkness, Mike gazed with interest at the indistinct figure.

SOLITARY TREE

When the latecomer emerged from the murky shadows into the light. Mike instantly recognized the petite figure of Mel.

Rising from his seated position Mike welcomed Melody Dawn Webster to his home, following a brief hug, Mike advised her that he had called her office, but was told she was on an extended personal leave.

"Yes, I had some personal issues that needed to be taken care of," explained Mel. "I had left a note with the receptionist though to contact me if you called."

"Would you like to go in and join the party?" asked Mike.

Smiling, she thanked Mike for his invitation, but declined stating. "It's been a rough month Mike, I just wanted to stop by and congratulate you on acquiring your house."

Thinking quickly Mike asked her if she liked Barbecued Steak and Baked Potato.

Placing her tiny hand lightly onto Mike's arm, she informed him that those two items were her favorites.

"Good it's settled then!" declared Mike. "How about you and me having dinner here tomorrow night."

"I would enjoy that," replied a somber Mel.

As Mike, escorted Mel back to her car, he thanked her for coming and told her that he was looking forward to tomorrow night.

Deciding that he was ready to once again brave the crowd in his house, Mike re-joined the party and attempted to say all the right things to all the right people. Busy shaking hands, exchanging anecdotes about police work with people he barely knew, Mike was amazed that the evening sped by so quickly. Stealing a quick unobtrusive glance at his watch, he was amazed to see that it was two o'clock in the morning as he and Yolanda ushered the last person from the house. Watching Yolanda as she began to gather her things, Mike insisted that given the time she was more than welcome to sleep in the master bedroom, he would be happy to sleep downstairs.

"You don't have to sleep downstairs," remarked Yolanda with an inviting look.

SOLITARY TREE

Gazing fondly at Yolanda, Mike knew what had been offered and so chose his words carefully. "Yolanda, I think I do need to sleep downstairs, I'm not sure what we might have, if indeed we have anything. But I would much rather sleep downstairs tonight rather than run the risk of screwing up what we now enjoy."
"May I speak bluntly Mike?"
"Of course," returned Mike.
"Your ex-wife has absolutely no fucking idea what she has lost! You are truly a gentleman, you are the type of man that young girls fantasize about marrying and having children with," as tears filled her eyes and spilled over onto her cheeks, she hugged Mike, and headed to the master bedroom.
Rising early the next morning, Mike donned an old pair of black sweat pants, and a ragged T-shirt, that he found hidden under the bed, from when he had been the tenant, and not the owner of the house. He set about cleaning up the wreckage left from the night before, never been one to host parties even when married to Adele, he felt that last night was a success due wholly to Yolanda's Herculean efforts.
With his arms, up to his elbows in soapy water, scrubbing the last remaining pot Mike was surprised to hear his doorbell ring. Wiping the residual water and soap suds off his arms, Mike opened his front door to see a young man standing on the porch.
At first glance Mike thought it must be Halloween, as this young man's face was festooned with metal. He had metal rings in his lips, metal studs protruding from his cheeks, completing the collection with a golden ring in his nose. It was then Mike noticed his hair, he had both sides of his scalp shaved clean with a strip of hair running down the center from which protruded six points of hair that closely resembled daggers.
"Good morning sir, my name is Richard, I am here to pick up some pots that Claude had left here."
Handing Richard, the box that contained the pots, Mike was about to close the door when Richard passed an envelope to Mike explaining the bill was inside.

SOLITARY TREE

Laughing out loud Richard also informed Mike that if he didn't pay the bill Claude knows where he lives.

"Ha Ha, ya that's funny alright," groused Mike as he closed the door, throwing the envelope onto his kitchen counter, Mike continued his cleaning regime.

Shortly after ten o'clock Yolanda breezed into the kitchen where Mike was still busy cleaning.

Wishing Mike a good morning, and wearing a small sheepish smile, readily admitted that her dress looked better worn at night to parties, then at ten o'clock in the morning the day after.

Mike judicially informed her that it didn't matter what time of day she wore the dress, she still looked fabulous.

Blushing slightly, Yolanda thanked him for being so gracious then declined his offer of a coffee, informing Mike that she needed to get going.

Escorting her to the front door, Mike gave her a quick hug and thanked her for all her hard work, telling her he thought the party had been a huge success. Watching Yolanda as she walked down the sidewalk towards her vehicle, Mike knew that he had taken the high road by sleeping downstairs, but that didn't mean he didn't regret that decision.

Two hours later, with the house once again returned to normal, Mike went shopping for that night's supper.

Having placed two foil wrapped potatoes on the barbecue, Mike had just sat down in a deck chair to relax when he heard his doorbell chime.

Opening the door, he was somewhat nervous as he greeted Melanie Webster, this nervousness was quickly dispelled when she moved close to Mike and gave him a quick hug. Turning slightly to allow Mel to move past him, Mike's attention was suddenly diverted as his eyes caught sight of a vaguely familiar figure furtively slipping out of sight behind a tree across the street. Not wanting to alarm Mel, he quickly ushered her into the kitchen, telling her to make herself to home as he needed to take care of something.

SOLITARY TREE

Stopping at the hall closet, Mike hastily removed his weapon from the lock box it's kept in, opening his front door he raced out to the street. Scanning the street in both directions he searched in vain for the familiar figure of Larry Donovan, Mike began to walk towards the tree that he was sure Larry had disappeared behind. Remembering that his weapon was in full view of anyone that might happen to be watching, Mike placed the weapon in the small of his back where his belt would hold it snugly in position, pulling his sweater down slightly to cover it. Having looked behind the tree, and several other possible hiding places with no sign of Larry, Mike decided to head back to his house and the waiting Melanie.

Striding past the parked cars on the street, Mike was just about to turn into his driveway when the heavily tinted driver's side window of a parked car silently descended.

Mike was thoroughly pissed off when he saw the smiling face of Scarface sitting behind the wheel of the car.

"What the fuck are you doing here?" growled Mike.

"Ki ordered me to come here to keep you safe," replied Scarface completely unruffled in the face of Mike's obvious anger.

"You can tell Ki that I am a grown boy, and certainly do not need his personal body guard hanging around my house!"

"Ki thinks you do. It would appear that Mr. Donovan is back in town and has been making threats against you."

Aware of the passing minutes and the fact that Melanie was waiting at the house, Mike informed Scarface that if he failed to leave the area immediately Mike would call the cops and report a suspicious vehicle.

Not waiting for a response from Scarface, Mike headed into his driveway, smiling as he heard Scarface's vehicle start, then quickly accelerate away.

SOLITARY TREE

Returning his weapon to the lockbox Mike called for Melanie, upon hearing her response from the area of the deck in the backyard Mike made his way to his backyard deck.

Apologizing for his erratic behavior, Mike assured her that all was well, pointing out that as the neighbors know he is a cop they are always telling him about suspicious looking people.

Indicating the two cold beers on the wooden picnic table, Melanie hoped that Mike didn't mind the fact that she had gone ahead and opened them.

"Not at all Mel," smiled Mike as he picked up both chilled bottles, handing one to Mel he then gently touched his bottle to hers expressing a small cheer.

Mel politely accepted Mike's offer of a quick tour of the house, placing the beverages back on the table Mike proudly showed off his home to her. When they entered the kitchen, Mel stared at the two place settings already in place at the kitchen table, turning her attention back to Mike, she studied him thoughtfully before speaking. "Correct me if I'm wrong, but I believe those places are set by a loving father who desperately wants to see his two daughters sitting there."

Turning away from Mel in a futile attempt at hiding his emotions, Mike leaned on the kitchen counter and stared out the large kitchen window at nothing. When he finally answered, her it was his fragmented voice that betrayed his inner turmoil. Mike's emotional state was manifested by his trembling shoulders, Melanie gently placed her hand on Mike's back and let her head rest against his bicep. She stood quietly there beside Mike, until she felt his trembling slowly begin to subside, then wanting to save him any possible embarrassment, she patted him gently on his back and murmured that she will be on the deck.

SOLITARY TREE

   With his emotions once again in check, Mike removed the two
marinated T-bone steaks from the refrigerator and made his way
out to the deck. Placing the platter of meat on the side table of
his barbecue, Mike sat down at the picnic table opposite Melanie
and meeting her gaze apologized for his melt down.
   "There is absolutely no need for you to apologize to me or to
anyone!" insisted Melanie. With these words, Melanie reached
across the table and resting her dainty hands on Mike's large
warm hands, expressed her passionate belief that one-day Mike
will find his daughters.
   "Thank-you for that Melanie," Mike replied soberly.
   Enquiring how Melanie liked her steak cooked, Mike made
himself busy as he introduced the refrigerated steaks to the
searing heat of the barbecue. As the aroma of grilling meat
immediately permeated the air, Mike gave the steaks a quick flip
to sear the opposite side before turning back to Melanie. He was
shocked as he observed huge tears slowly wending their way
down her face, yet at the same time she was smiling.
   Instantly alarmed at what he was observing, Mike asked her if
she was alright.
   "Is this allowed?" pondered Melanie.
   "I apologize Melanie, but I'm not sure what you mean," replied
Mike with a perplexed look on his face at this abrupt turn in the
conversation.
   "Is this allowed?" repeated Mel staring at Mike through her
tears. "This is all I have ever wanted, what we have right here
right now! What makes being happy so unattainable?"
   Unsure of where this conversation was headed, Mike could only
shrug his shoulders helplessly.
   It was at this point that Melanie launched into an explanation of
why she had taken an extended leave from her work.

SOLITARY TREE

"I had an identical twin sister, her name was Jolene, and I hated her," confessed Melanie. "My parents idolized her, she was so full of life, she was the popular one, the one that everyone invited to parties. She was incredibly intelligent, where I would have to study to pass tests in school, she hardly opened her books and yet was still able to ace her exams."

Re-claiming his seat across the table from Melanie, Mike's attention was riveted on her as she continued.

"Unfortunately, Jolene was also an addict. Some asshole introduced her to drugs when we were teenagers, our parents had her admitted to numerous Re-Hab clinics over the years but the successes were always short lived. Unfortunately, she shared a needle with someone who was infected with HIV, Jolene was never one to see a doctor, and by the time she finally figured out that she was seriously ill it was too late. She was placed on a regimen of drugs, but because she had chosen to ignore her condition for so long, the medications only bought her a short reprieve.

At this juncture, Mike rose from his seat to flip the grilling steaks, and retrieved a bottle of red wine from the kitchen along with a couple of light crystal, wine glasses. With each glass, half full, Mike quietly passed one to Melanie, then regaining his seat waited for Melanie to continue.

Thanking Mike, Melanie picked up her narrative where she had left off. "I have spent this past month with my sister, cursing the disease that was killing her, and despising myself for ever being so petty that I had resented the attention she craved. Everyone claims that twins share a special bond, I would beg to differ, but now I wonder was that my fault, or hers? When she died, I was hugging her begging her to hang on, she opened her eyes one last time, whispered that she loved me, but said she had to go."

Excusing himself, Mike slipped quickly into the house and grabbed a sweater for Melanie along with a box of Kleenex, placing the sweater on her shoulders to fend off the early evening chill, he was rewarded with a warm smile of gratitude.

SOLITARY TREE

Taking a small sip of wine Melanie continued. "I never attended her funeral, instead I bought a great bottle of wine, went to a local beach that I knew was rarely visited, sat on the rocks and consumed the wine. When the bottle was empty, I began walking into the ocean, the water was ice cold, I walked until I could walk no longer, I then started swimming. I thought that if I kept swimming until I could swim no more than I could join my sister." With one swallow Melanie emptied her glass and concluded her narrative. "I would like to think that my sister saved me, but in all honesty, I believe I was too cowardly to actually commit suicide. I made my way back to shore, exhausted I fell asleep right there on the beach, and ironically would have died of hypothermia were it not for the timely intervention of a homeless beachcomber who happened by. Therefore, I wonder; do we need to feel pain to acknowledge the fact we're alive? Why can't we feel happiness to achieve the same end? Is there any hope for people like us to experience happiness?

Observing the tear-filled eyes of Melanie, Mike acknowledged the fact that he too had almost given up on finding happiness, but he had since learned that happiness is subjective, it is also fleeting, he attempted to explain to Melanie that at this very moment in time, he was happier than he had been in a very long time. He cannot begin to come close to finding the right words to describe the happiness he was feeling that Melanie was still alive. "Happiness is an elusive concept, best accepted in small portions, as opposed to looking for the three-course meal," concluded Mike pensively.

"So, there is hope for us," whispered Melanie.

Standing up Mike held out his hand to Melanie in a silent invitation, grasping the proffered hand Melanie moved with Mike to the sliding glass doors that led from the deck into the kitchen, pointing to the kitchen table with the two-place settings for his daughters, Mike declared he will never give up hope.

SOLITARY TREE

Emotionally drained after her soul baring monologue, Melanie was only able to eat a small portion of supper, before taking her leave.

Clearing away the few dishes, Mike was thankful that Melanie had not been able to end her life, and fervently hoped that at some point in time they will discover happiness.

.

CHAPTER TEN

"The Captain wants to see you!"

With his head buried in paperwork Mike did not need to look up to see who it was that possessed the temerity to issue that terse order. Sure enough, when Mike finally did look up he was not surprised to see the lean, raptor like countenance of Lieutenant Bowers glaring at him.

Holding up his hand as though warding off the obvious question, Bowers informed Mike that he was to report to the Captains office immediately.

As the Captain's secretary ushered him into the inner sanctum, Mike was instantly aware of the fact that this was not going to be a pleasant meeting. Not looking up from what he was occupied with, the captain silently pointed in the direction of a chair.

With a sense of foreboding Mike sat down on the unforgiving, hard wooden straight backed chair that he's becoming very familiar with. Mike spent the next five minutes in uncomfortable silence awaiting the captains pleasure.

Finally, the Captain appeared to complete the task he was absorbed in, Mike watched as he carefully placed his pen in its holder then lifted his head and glared at Mike without a shred of warmth emanating from his cold blue eyes.

In a voice that was glacial cold, he quietly informed Mike that he had just endured a forty-five-minute harangue from the Feds.

"Now I want you to tell me why in the fuck you've not mentioned to me the fact that Ki Chiang Yee is your fucking uncle!"

SOLITARY TREE

Taken aback by the hostility present in the Captain's voice, Mike imparted the same information to the captain that he had given the three feds. Mike also re-affirmed the fact that he had been eight years old the last time he had set eyes on Ki.

As he listened to Mike's explanation about being related to the notorious Ki, and the fact that Mike unfortunately had no control over who his relatives were, the Captain appeared to slowly thaw out.

When Mike had finished his explanation, the Captain continued to stare at Mike over the span of several heartbeats before he continued in a slightly less hostile voice. "So why would Special Agent Stefaniski ask me to initiate a complaint of assault against you?"

Maintaining the same neutral tone of voice, Mike explained to the Captain the events that led up to his attack on Stefaniski.

Nodding his head as he heard Mike's rendition of the story, the Captain smiled warmly when Mike described the part when he had straightened Stefaniski's tie.

"All that aside Mike, I'm still bothered by the fact that you did not inform me of your familial ties to Ki however distant they may in fact be. The Feds have requested that I remove you from your current position," holding up a hand to ward off Mike's protest the captain continued. "I have never liked the Feds, and if they think they can come in here and tell me how to do my job they are sadly mistaken. My confidence in your ability to fulfill your duties has not been altered, but having said that, we will need to carefully consider our options. If the media were to learn of this, they would have a field day, just imagine the headlines Chief of Detectives related to Chinese crime boss. The Feds also put forth the suggestion that you insert yourself into Ki's organization, and supply them with credible evidence of Ki's illegal activities."

It was this last suggestion that caused Mike to squirm uncomfortably on the hard chair.

SOLITARY TREE

"Captain, maybe you and the Feds are missing the point that Ki would kill me as quick as anyone else. He would feel absolutely no remorse in doing so, the fact that we are related means nothing to him. He has this delusional idea that he is some sort of feudal Khan. The terrifying part is, he believes that he is a Khan, and as such, has the power of life and death over the people he refers to as his subjects."

"Are you fearful of him?" enquired the captain.

"With all due respect sir, only an idiot wouldn't be scared!" declared Mike bluntly.

Leaning back in his chair, the captain carefully scrutinized Mike for any outward signs of nervousness. "Mike, bear with me while I put forth a hypothetical situation," he continued to scrutinize Mike, like a cat would an unsuspecting rodent, before attacking. "What if Ki had something over you, something that he could use to gain information from you, concerning any investigations of ours into his business dealings."

Upon hearing these words uttered by the captain, Mike willfully restrained himself from swallowing, which is often construed as a sign of nervousness. He then decided that it was time to go on the offensive. Sitting forward in the chair, Mike glared at the captain, and for the next three minutes unleashed a torrent of angry rhetoric. "Again, with all due respect sir, if that is how you feel then it shows you have a piss poor ability to judge people. For fuck's sake, I did not come looking for this position, you approached me, on the day that this position was offered to me I thought I was being fired!" With his pulse, clearly visible in the vein protruding from the left side of his neck, Mike reached for the pad of paper that was situated on the captain's desk, plucking a pen from his shirt pocket he began writing.

"What is that?" demanded the captain.

"My fuckin resignation, Sir!" blazed Mike, the emphasis on the sir flirting with sarcastic insubordination. Forcefully ripping the sheet of paper from the pad Mike tossed it in the general direction of the captain.

SOLITARY TREE

Picking up the paper the captain read out loud what Mike had written.

"I Mike Chance, do hereby quit my fuckin job as Chief of Detectives, this is to be effective immediately. Well Mike," stated the captain with a wry smile. "This is not exactly a classic example of an eloquently written resignation, but it can be torn up in the same fashion as if you had spent a full day composing one," where upon the captain proceeded to tear the page in half, then leaned over and deposited the unaccepted resignation into his garbage receptacle.

"Now that we have the anger out of the way Mike, perhaps we can allow cooler heads to prevail. Let me reiterate, my confidence in you is unshaken, I was surprised at learning your kinship to Ki, but as you have explained, an accident of birth is certainly beyond your control. The problem we face is, how do we mitigate any collateral damage that may occur if the media should learn of this. For now, this will be kept confidential, but in the meantime, we need to throw the Feds a bone," smiling as an idea suddenly occurred to him, the captain closed his eyes for a brief period while he appeared to mull over his idea.

Opening his eyes, he stated unequivocally. "This is what we will do, I will inform the Feds that we need time to devise a game plan that would allow you to gain Ki's trust. I will also inform them that if the media should learn about your relationship with Ki, by any other source then my office then the deal falls off the table."

"That sounds fine Sir, but at some point, in time the Feds will expect me to do something towards that end," rebutted Mike.

"Yes Mike, I concur with your synopsis, but this would buy us time to break the news to the media through a reporter I know personally, and who happens to be a friend of the Department."

Standing up the captain indicated the meeting was concluded by extending his right hand, Mike quickly rose and shook the offered hand, with the captain once again re-affirming his confidence in Mike.

PART TWO

CHAPTER ELEVEN

Hearing her five-year-old sister Sandra, begin to cry in her bed, seven-year-old Jasmine quickly slipped from her own bed slipped across the room and knelt beside her bed. "Sandra," hissed Jasmine, deliberately keeping her voice discreet so their parents didn't hear them. "You have to stop crying! Do you want that horrible man to come back and take us away again?"

"Why are you calling me Sandra? My name is Maebel," she cried.

"Not anymore!" declared Jasmine. "Please Sandra," begged Jasmine. "You have to stop crying or else we will be taken away again like the last time. Jackie and Barry seem to be nice, and they treat us like their own children," entreated a desperate Jasmine.

"I want my real Mommy and Daddy," blubbered an inconsolable Sandra.

"So do I," professed Jasmine. "But they died in the car accident, so now we have Jackie and Barry."

With her sobs beginning to subside, Sandra asked her sister. "So where did Maebel go? Did she die like Mommy and Daddy? Do you think she's with Mommy and Daddy right now?"

"No silly she didn't die. You were Maebel and you're still here with me, you just have a different name now like me, I used to be called Jessica, now they say my name is Jasmine."

"These people talk so fast they sound funny," murmured Sandra.

Displaying a small smile that went unnoticed in the dark room, Jasmine silently agreed whole heartedly with her sister's statement.

SOLITARY TREE

Hearing approaching footsteps, Jasmine quickly placed a small kiss on her sister's cheek and launched herself across the room into her own bed, barely having time to bury herself under the blankets before the door opened.

Jasmine need not to have worried about her sister's crying, as it appeared the threat of that horrible man returning to take them away, caused Sandra to control her emotions.

"Are they asleep?" queried Barry looking up from his newspaper as his wife Jackie returned to the den.

"Yes, they are, I thought I heard Sandie crying, so I looked in on them and they're both fast asleep," replied Jackie relaxing in her favorite chair.

Staring thoughtfully at her husband of eight years Jackie asked him. "Is what we did actually legal Barry?"

Thinking that her husband had not heard her, Jackie was about to re-iterate her question when Barry shuffled his newspaper and placed it on the nearby coffee table.

"What do you mean?" Barry asked quietly.

"Well, I have been thinking, paying money to that creepy looking Dan seemed wrong, it felt like we bought the girls."

"Our lawyer Giles Bendicott, felt the same way as you do, he advised me against moving forward with the adoption. He felt that from a legal perspective there were too many unanswered questions, the answers he could get, were vague to say the least. But, I ask you this Jackie, could you have left those two beautiful young girls with that guy, if I did not fear for the girl's safety I would have had the police all over him. I was willing to sell off all our assets, if necessary to save them. Now we have the family we have always wanted, we have two gorgeous daughters that are named after our mothers, we will raise these two girls like our own, hopefully they will learn to love us as the only parents they will have ever known."

SOLITARY TREE

"I can't help but wonder about the circumstances that allowed that man to become the girl's legal representative," pondered Jackie.

"Life is not always fair Jackie; we do what we can, when we can. We have been told that the girl's parents were killed in a car crash, so we have no choice but to accept that explanation. To waste time and resources ascertaining if that is true or not would be pointless. Let's look to the future and not the past."

With those words being spoken, the girls fate was sealed, they would be brought up in the bourgeoning community of Vernon, British Columbia, with parents Barry and Jackie Wentworth.

Barry and Jackie were teenagers the first time they met at the local fall fair. Barry at eighteen years old had communicated to his dad that very night, he had met the girl he was going to marry. Jackie on the other hand, adamantly declared to her friends that she was not in the least bit interested in Barry. And so, began the courtship that lasted seven years ending in a wedding surrounded by friends and family.

Barry had spent four years away from home while he obtained his college degree in Business Management, while co-incidentally Jackie had spent four years at the same institution obtaining her Diploma as a Registered Nurse.

Returning home together with their respective degrees, the community of Vernon was not surprised when wedding invitations were soon arriving in the mail.

Barry was average in just about everything, five feet ten inches tall, slight build, unruly, sandy colored hair with an easy smile, which combined with a highly contagious laugh had people constantly gravitate towards him at social events. It was his business acumen that set him far above others, he possessed the uncanny ability to ascertain successful business opportunities that others were blind to.

Jackie at five feet two inches, was constantly at war with her weight.

SOLITARY TREE

She used to enjoy a head of long, thick, wavy brunette hair, but had since learned that short hair is much easier to deal with when nursing was your chosen career.

  Settling into the routine of married life, Barry would concentrate on acquiring several businesses, while at the same time Jackie was working long hours as a Registered Nurse at the local hospital.

  Weary of living in the cramped quarters of their tiny apartment, one cold, wet, Saturday morning they went for a drive-in search of alternative living accommodations. Spotting a real estate sign advertising an open house they decided to go have a quick look. The five-bedroom home nestled on the shores of beautiful Kal Lake, was exactly what they were looking for, watching the gamut of expressions cross his wife's face while they toured the incredible home with all its spacious rooms, he realized that returning to living in a cramped apartment was out of the question.

  After lengthy negotiations with the owners of the house, and long, and at times heated meetings with a local banking institution, the dream of owning the house on Kal Lake came to fruition.

  Barry was beside himself with joy as he watched his wife's reaction as they walked for the first time, through the doorway of their home as the new owners. Jackie quickly went about the business of making the nest their own, marching through each room with a handful of paint swatches, she carefully chose colors that would best suit the room. Observing his wife and her obvious delight with her new task, Barry knew that he would do everything in his power to ensure her happiness.

  With the house completely re-decorated and furnished to Jackie's satisfaction, the expected announcement of being pregnant was not forthcoming. At first this missing, fundamental component of their marriage was blamed on busy lives and stress.

SOLITARY TREE

 However, as the years quickly sped by with still no children's shrieks of joy at Christmas time, or quiet dinners listening to their children talk about school, Jackie began to grow impatient.

 After pouring a small amount of red wine for herself and Barry from a world renowned local winery, Jackie exited the house and joined her husband on the large sundeck that overlooked the shimmering vista of Kal Lake. Though they had now lived here for several years, they never grew tired of the of the natural beauty. On the East side of the Lake, the almost vertical slope of heavily forested, pristine hills stood guard against further human encroachment, while on the West side of the lake were the rolling grasslands so prevalent to this area, on any given day one could spot semi-wild horses, along with just as wild cattle, slowly grazing. It was the shimmering Emerald color of the waters of Kal Lake that first captured tourist's attention, they would gather at several high vantage points to gaze at the Lake's unique color. Enjoying the quiet solitude of the warm summer evening, Barry and Jackie sat in companionable silence, watching as two kayakers glided silently by, with their paddle's rhythmic strokes reflecting the slow descent of the setting sun.

 "It's too quiet," commented Jackie.

 "Not really," laughed Barry softly. "It's nice when us locals get a chance to enjoy looking at the lake without the tourists and their noisy boats racing all over it."

 "True, but they do bring their money with them, and even better they leave once school starts again," stated a smiling Jackie as she sipped her wine thoughtfully. "That wasn't exactly what I was referring to though Barry, we enjoy an incredible marriage, right this very minute we have everything that anyone could possibly want, except children. I'm not sure why we can't get pregnant, perhaps we need to have some tests done to ascertain why we are unable to conceive."

SOLITARY TREE

Placing his now empty wine glass on the small, round glass top table beside his deck chair, Barry reached across the short span that separated himself and Jackie, and gently grasped one of her small hands with his own.

"If that is what you think we need to do, then fine let's do it," Barry responded. "But, I would like you to consider this. We have been married for six years now, and we have thus far been unsuccessful at being able to fill our home with children. So, I believe we have two choices open to us, we could subject ourselves to a battery of tests regarding not only the physical aspects of our marriage, but as well I'm sure they would like to explore the mental state of our marriage.

We are two normal, healthy adults who unfortunately have been unable to conceive, do we want to subject ourselves to that type of scrutiny?" Continuing to hold his wife's hand, Barry paused while he gathered his thoughts before beginning again.

"If by chance the doctors do discover that one of us might have a physical impairment that inhibits getting pregnant, this could possibly cause some form of resentment. So, I would like to propose that we look at adoption, tragically, the children that are classed as wards of the Government number in the thousands. They range in age from newborn right up to eighteen years old."

"You really feel that way Barry?" questioned Jackie as she studied her husband. "You would be willing to raise somebody else's children as though they were your own."

"Of course I would Jackie, they would be our legal children, sure someone else was responsible for their genetics, but we would have the pleasure of watching them grow into adults."

As Jackie mulled over what her husband had said, she slowly started to nod her head in agreement, having never given adoption much consideration, assuming they would one day have their own children.

Smiling at her husband, Jackie informed him that the hospital has a children's welfare representative on staff that she would talk to tomorrow.

SOLITARY TREE

Pointing in the direction of his empty glass, Jackie enquired if he would like a little wine to celebrate this new direction they were going to take.

Nodding his head in assent, Barry watched his beautiful wife gather the two glasses and head inside the house, he was never going to impart to her that fearful he might be responsible for the lack of children, had presented himself to a private clinic for testing. The results of the test had shown beyond a doubt, that he possessed the capabilities of impregnating a female.

"Seven years!" wailed a distraught Jackie to her husband Barry, as he walked into their house the night following their discussion about adopting children.

"It can take up to seven years to get approval to adopt children," she explained bitterly to her husband.

While Barry made them each a cocktail, then carried them out onto the deck, Jackie continued to be-moan the fact that in seven years they would be too old, and no child in their right mind would want to be placed with old people.

Realizing that attempting to placate his wife at this point would be futile, Barry continued to listen to her vent about the injustice of having people wait seven years.

As Jackie's tirade against all Government agencies, and their idiotic rules began to run out of steam, Barry smiled as she finally stopped to take a sip of her cocktail.

"Finished now?" asked a smiling Barry.

"For now," admitted Jackie allowing a small smile to appear at the corners of her mouth adding. "I guess I was a little worked up."

"Just a little Jackie," agreed Barry. He explained to Jackie, that he had also spent some time that day investigating the whole adoption issue. The government had not, as far as Barry could tell changed their approach to adoption in the last thirty-five years.

SOLITARY TREE

Knowing full well her husband's bull- dog like tenacity once he commits to a project, Jackie continued to listen closely to what he was saying.

"This is a new world that we live in, unfortunately our Government is somehow oblivious to this fact.

With the whole world, literally at our fingertips through the internet, we could if we so desired adopt a child from any nation in the world in a matter of weeks, versus years. I met with Giles today and we formulated a plan that I would like to explain to you." Barry went on to describe to her about a website that he and Giles had located that had many kids ready for adoption. "As we speak Giles is investigating the legality of the company, the gentleman who seems to be the President of this agency will be in this area in two days' time with two girls that are ready to be adopted.

CHAPTER TWELVE

Two days later when Barry's cell phone indicated a call from an unknown source, he felt an immediate spike in his blood pressure, knowing that they were about to take an irrevocable step. Upon finding out the location where he was to meet Dan Fraser and his two young charges, Barry immediately contacted Jackie and informed her of the time and place. He then placed a call to his lawyer Giles to ensure he would also be present at the meeting.

Meeting Jackie outside the rather rundown, and somewhat time worn Traveler's Motel on Twelfth Street, the withering look he received from his wife over the location of this meeting clearly displayed her skepticism. She was about to voice her concerns when Giles pulled into the parking lot, parking his vehicle he joined his anxious looking clients.

Glancing around at the grim looking premises Giles muttered jokingly to Barry. "I didn't think that we would require a Police presence."

"Well he said room Two-Ten, I guess we should probably use the stairs," commented Barry, smiling as he attempted to ease their misgivings.

SOLITARY TREE

Ascending the stairs, they soon located the room they were
seeking, Giles tapped Barry lightly on his shoulder indicating the
window's curtains were closed, at the same time pointing to the
bright daylight, it was easy to see that Giles was becoming
apprehensive.

Ignoring Giles's obvious concerns Barry knocked loudly on the
door, the trio immediately heard a harsh sounding adult male
voice ordering someone to behave, and for Christ sakes smile.

A rather non-descript, nervous looking individual opened the
door and introduced himself to the trio as Dan Fraser.

As they swiftly absorbed the physical details of Dan, the
greasy, thinning blonde hair with a bad comb over, the washed
out blue eyes that looked like they had difficulty focusing,
combined with the purple tinged nose of a hard drinker, they're
apprehension concerning the legitimacy of this event quickly
escalated.

Giles stepped forward and introduced himself, advising Dan that
he was legal counsel for the Wentworth's, whilst he attempted to
peer into the gloom of the darkened room.

Realizing that he may have unwittingly placed his wife in what
might very well become a dangerous situation, Barry marched
uninvited into the room opened the closed window curtains and
turned on the light. Turning back to Dan, he brusquely informed
him that if the children were not immediately produced, they
were going to leave.

Sensing that Barry was not about to be placated by words, Dan
glared at him while he sidled past and opened the bathroom door
ordering the two people inside to come out.

With downcast eyes and tightly clasped hands, the two young
girls left the confines of the small bathroom, as the light from the
window shone on the girls there was an audible gasp from
Jackie.

With her maternal instincts, instantly aroused, she elbowed Dan
aside as she moved swiftly to encompass the girls in a hug.

SOLITARY TREE

"How could you?" Jackie hissed venomously at Dan, "When was the last time these poor girls had a bath, look at their hair, it doesn't look like it's seen a comb in a week." Picking up the smaller girl, and taking the slightly bigger girl by the hand, Jackie informed Barry as she marched from the room, that he will do whatever it took to ensure these poor girls go home with them.

The first month as a family of four sped by so quickly for the Wentworth's, it's like it never happened. With no small amount of trepidation Barry and Jackie, along with their lawyer presented themselves at the local courthouse to initiate the process of having the girl's names changed. Both Barry and Jackie sighed out loud with relief, as the documents that Dan had supplied concerning the girl's background, appeared to raise no questions from the bored looking records clerk.

There were appointments with the family physician, to ascertain the state of the girl's health. Jackie and Barry were relieved to hear that the girl's general physical health seemed to be fine, the doctor though confessed that in his opinion, Sandie appeared to display behavioral patterns often related to stress, or anxiety. When Jackie and Barry informed their doctor that Sandie peed the bed quite often, he was not at all surprised and told them that with time, and a secure family life this should remedy itself. There were trips to the dentist where they discovered that Jasmine required another appointment to fill three small cavities. Not surprisingly, when Barry had requested his lawyer Giles, to contact Dan Fraser with respect to the girl's education status, Giles reported back to Barry that all attempts to reach Dan had failed. The now effervescent Jackie contacted the local School District, and explained to them the situation regarding the girl's education status. The School District informed her they would send an educational professional, who would give the girls some simple tests to discover their capabilities.

SOLITARY TREE

On the September morning that Jasmine was about to begin Grade one, Jackie was surprised when she entered the girl's bedroom to see Sandie standing in the middle of the room crying.

"Oh Honey! What's the matter?" enquired an immediately concerned Jackie.

"I wet the bed!" wailed an extremely distraught Sandie.

Surprised at this revelation since it had been quite a while since Sandie had peed the bed, Jackie quickly consoled the upset Sandie and began to rid her of the cold, wet, smelly pajamas.

"Are you going to send me away?" whimpered Sandie.

Embracing the forlorn looking Sandie, wet pajama's and all, Jackie quickly consoled her. "Honey, we would never send you away, you and your sister are our family now."

"You're sending Jas away today," bawled Sandie.

It was this statement of Sandie's, that brought realization to Jackie concerning the wet bed.

"No Sweetie. We aren't sending Jas away. She's just going to start school and will return this afternoon," Jackie reassured her youngest daughter.

"You're sure!" asked a tearful Sandie.

"Positive," stated Jackie and bestowing a love filled hug upon her removed the wet pajamas.

Thus, began saga of the Wentworth family, the first of what would be many milestones with this family, occurred after the girls had been living with Jackie and Barry for just about a year.

On a Saturday morning like any other Saturday morning, Sandie who appeared to be still half asleep, walked into the kitchen where Barry and Jackie were seated at the kitchen table enjoying a cup of coffee, sat herself down at the table, poured a bowl of cereal, and casually announced for the first time. "Morning Mom and Dad."

SOLITARY TREE

Both parents were thunderstruck by this casual announcement, not wanting to embarrass Sandie with an emotional outpouring, they responded in kind, wishing her a good morning, but as the silently jubilant parents exchanged glances it was easy to see their eyes shining with unshed tears of happiness.

A few minutes later, a disheveled looking Jas made her entrance in to the kitchen, bestowing a hug first upon Jackie then made her way to Barry, after which she sat down at the table, and just as casually as her sister did previously, addressed Jackie and Barry, as Mom and Dad.

This marked the end of the tenuous, and somewhat precarious relationship that had existed between the two girls and their parents, making way for a healthy relationship to evolve in its stead.

The only shadow on the horizon appeared in the form of Barry's eight-year-old nephew. When Barry and Jackie held a family get together to formally announce that the girls name change was now legal, and introduce them to their cousins, Barry's eight-year-old nephew Bradley, who was never one to give up the limelight easily, called the girls outsiders, adding thinly veiled remarks that could easily be construed as racist, concerning the shape of the girl's eyes, and their skin-color.

Having never liked his spoiled, obnoxious, and often outspoken young nephew, Barry's patience had finally been exhausted with him. Exuding a calm demeanor that hid his inwardly seething anger, Barry calmly asked his brother Henry to gather up his family and please leave, and when Bradley had learned some manners they would be more than welcome back into Barry and Jackie's home.

CHAPTER THIRTEEN

As the months rolled into years, the Wentworth family grew stronger, and solidified into a tightly knit family unit. As Sandie and Jas matured, they shed their childish good looks, and became strikingly attractive teenagers.

At fifteen years of age Jas was now a full five inches taller than her mother Jackie, she retained her exquisitely long, jet black hair. She was highly popular in school, never lacking invitations to attend social events, this however never interfered with her unwavering dedication to attaining the highest grades possible. Jas had steadfastly maintained for several years that she wanted to be a Health Care Professional, her capacity for caring for others was unfathomable.

Sandie on the other hand at thirteen years old was still awaiting a growth spurt, she had opted for short hair that bonded tightly to her head. With the identical black eyes of her sister, and their shared toffee colored skin they were easily the most attractive girls in their middle school. Although headed in a different direction then her sister, Sandie's dedication to her schoolwork was equal to that of Jas. Sandie had at an early age formed a bond with Kal Lake, with her parents' house situated on the shores of the lake it seemed only natural to become intrigued by the lake. Often, seated at the kitchen table that afforded a view of the lake, Sandie would be captivated by small uneven waves on the water, and briefly tearing her eyes away would soberly announce to her parents the lake was restless.

SOLITARY TREE

She had solemnly informed her parents that she will be a Marine Biologist, that there's a whole world of living creatures residing within the water that we have no knowledge of.

With her expressed love of the lake it was never hard to find Sandie, whenever she had a free moment she could be found at the end of her parents sixty-foot dock, with a Fly-Rod in her hands, a special gift from her late grandfather.

On a warm, sunny, Saturday morning in late April, Sandie was in her usual spot at the end of her parent's wharf with Fly-Rod in hand, attempting to fool the elusive Rainbow Trout. Although she did indeed love the art of Fly-Fishing, she loved the peace and tranquility it afforded, she had learned that for the most part if people saw you with a Fishing Rod they generally left you alone.

Barry's father Paul, an avid Fly-Fisherman, had despaired at the thought that he might not have the opportunity to pass on to the next generation his knowledge, and love, of the sport. However, when Sandie was ten years old she had watched her Grandpa Fly-Fishing, and became instantly captivated by the whole process, she bluntly demanded that he teach her. At first Paul, had thought that Sandie was simply humoring him, but when she refused to stop hounding him he realized that his wish had been granted. Three years later Sandie had become proficient at the sport, but most importantly had learned to release the fish she caught, with the same care shown by a nurse to a patient.

Not possessing the same extroverted personality of her sister, Sandie enjoyed time alone in which she allowed her mind to play back the events that have transpired in her young life. Feeling the vibrations of approaching footsteps reverberate through the roughhewn planks of the wharf, Sandie did not need to look to see who it was that had broken the universally accepted creed regarding fisherman.

"Hi Sandie," called out her approaching sister.

SOLITARY TREE

Turning to watch her sister approach, Sandie brushed aside the minor feeling of irritation she felt at Jas's interruption.

"Morning Jas. Just get up?" enquired Sandie as she executed another flawless cast with her Fly-Rod.

"No. I've been up for a while, Mom needed a hand to move some furniture around, so I volunteered since my sister was nowhere to be found," stated Jas with a smile that embodied the love she felt for her younger sister.

Sandie was not at all surprised at this revelation, for reasons that are known only to their Mom, she loved to move furniture around in the springtime.

"Sandie, why do you spend so much time fishing, yet you never keep any fish you catch?" asked Jas with a perplexed look.

Staring thoughtfully into the Green waters of Kal Lake, Sandie informed her sister that when a fish was caught, it became a test of wills between the Fisherman and the Fish, she patiently explained to her sister that releasing the fish with only it's pride injured, is a time-honored tradition with true sportsman.

With measured turns of her reel, Sandie eventually had her fly line once again nestled on the reel, gently placing the rod on the wharf, she joined her sister who had sat down on the roughhewn planks of the wharf. Gently moving her dangling legs back and forth, while staring into the depths of Kal Lake, a serious - minded Sandie asked Jas if she ever thought about their parents.

"Of course, I do silly, right now Mom is up there in the house moving things around, and Dad went into the office."

Staring at her sister Sandie clarified her question. "No I mean our birth parents; do you remember them?"

"What brought this on?" enquired Jas.

"I'm not sure," answered Sandie. "We have incredible parents that love us, and more importantly treat us as though we are their own children. It's just occasionally, I can't help but think about the other parents, and wonder what they were like."

SOLITARY TREE

"I know," responded a somber Jas. "There are times when I also wonder about them. I feel sad that I can't even remember their names, or what they looked like, it's as if they didn't exist," gazing at her younger sister Jas added. "I often wonder who we look like, do we look like our Dad or our Mom? Did we have grandparents that didn't want us?"

"We are so lucky that Mom and Dad adopted us, could you imagine growing up in an orphanage, that would have been awful!" shuddered Sandie with mock tremors.

Attempting to lighten the mood, Jas lightly tapped her sister on her bicep and replied. "Well we don't have to worry about that now do we. Hey, do you want to walk into town maybe go surprise Dad?"

Returning the tap on the bicep of Jas, Sandie was surprised to hear a small stifled groan of pain issued by her sister.

"Come on Jas, I never hit you that hard," chided a startled Sandie.

Rolling up her short-sleeved T-shirt, Jas exposed a nasty looking bruise that covered the entire area of her bicep.

"Holy Shit!" breathed Sandie as she gently ran her fingers over the affected area. "What the hell happened, sis?"

"Bradley did this," murmured Jas.

"Jesus Christ Jas! We should show Dad. That asshole is such a bully and a coward. Come on Jas get up; we're going to Dad's office."

With a reluctant Jas in tow, the two girls hurriedly covered the short distance into town, making their way to their Dad's office, where they found him wearing sweatpants, and ragged T-shirt watching Baseball on the large, flat screen TV located in his office.

Laughing uproariously at being caught by his daughters, Barry informed them that this was his way of avoiding their Mom's springtime furniture move.

Laughing along with their Dad, Sandie then turned serious and told Jas to show him her arm.

SOLITARY TREE

Revealing her arm, and the extent of the bruising, Barry was immediately contrite and asked Jas for an explanation.

As she re-counted the fact that their cousin Bradley had for no reason whatsoever, hit her the other day in school, Barry calmly told his girls to remain in the office and watch TV.

On the short drive, over to his brother Henry's residence, Barry silently acknowledged the fact that he had always considered Bradley to be a bully.

At seventeen years, old, Bradley was significantly bigger than most of his peer group, and rather than win respect by exhibiting kindness, he chose to use his physical presence to instill fear in others.

Turning his car onto the quiet residential street that his brother lived on, Barry was amused to see the target of his wrath on the large front lawn attempting to start a lawnmower. Bringing the car to an abrupt halt, Barry slammed the car's transmission into park and exited the vehicle.

Striding across the lawn, Barry had almost reached his nephew before Bradley sensing, he was not alone looked up.

"Hey, Uncle Barry, can you help me get this stupid lawnmower started?" enquired the frustrated Bradley.

Maintaining a stony silence, Barry simply walked up to his nephew, and without any warning punched him as hard as could on his nephew's right bicep, then calmly asked. "How the fuck does that feel asshole?"

"What the fuck? You crazy or what? Why the fuck did you do that?" moaned Bradley through clenched teeth as he massaged the injured area.

Waving his finger in Bradley's face, Barry warned him that in the future if Bradley even looked at Jas or Sandie, Barry would kick the shit out of him.

"You better watch out for that finger Uncle, you might just lose it," warned Bradley desperately attempting to inject bravado into his voice.

SOLITARY TREE

Upon hearing this threat Barry, unleashed a flurry of blows that had his nephew back- pedaling across the lawn so quickly that he fell backwards and landed on his ass.

"Get up you chicken shit son of a bitch," growled Barry. "You're bigger than I am, let's see how do against someone that will fight back."

The impact of Barry's fists on the face of his nephew, was clearly evidenced by the blood slowly trickling from his nostrils, along with highly visible red marks branded on his cheeks.

"Why did you hit me Uncle Barry?" whined Bradley with tears flowing from his eyes.

"Ya just what I thought. I always thought you were a coward and a bully," declared Barry in voice that did nothing to disguise the contempt he felt for his nephew.

It was at this juncture that Barry became aware of his slightly overweight, older brother Henry, still wearing his housecoat, approach rapidly from the direction of the house.

"What the fuck are you doing Barry?" bellowed a highly-agitated Henry. "I look out the window and I see you beating the shit out of my kid, you crazy or something?"

Staring at Bradley who was no longer openly crying, but was at the same time showing no inclination to standup, Barry ordered him to tell his dad what he did to Jas.

Looking completely confused by the events unfolding on his front lawn on a Saturday morning, Henry looked at his son and asked him for clarification.

"The other day in school I tapped Jas lightly on her arm. It was nothing, I barely even touched her," explained Bradley defending his actions. "Then this asshole showed up and sucker punched me."

"You hit your cousin Jas?" Henry shouted at his son. "You're fuckin lucky I didn't know of this first, or it would have been me kicking your ass down the street."

SOLITARY TREE

A bewildered Bradley, who minutes ago, thought his lifeline would be in the form of his Dad, realized that he was without allies.

"He's lucky this time Henry, I chose to settle this without involving the cops. If, there is a next time I will first kick the shit out of him, then I will have the cops charge him with assault," warned Barry quietly.

Nodding his head in assent, Henry echoed his brother's words adding. "I would gladly kick his ass all the way to the police station," growled Henry glaring at his son. "There is no excuse whatsoever for raising a hand to a female, this will not be tolerated. I will take you over to your Uncle's so you can apologize to Jas."

Entering his office with Henry and Bradley, Barry informed Jas, that Bradley wished to apologize.

Staring at her cousin with thinly concealed loathing Jas spoke up. "Bradley everyone at school knows you're a bully and a coward, I don't want your apology as that would be meaningless, what I want you to do is wear a pink shirt to school for a week in support of anti-bullying."

"I'm not wearing a pink shirt for anyone," growled Bradley sullenly.

Delivering a cuff to the side of Bradley's head, Henry informed his son that they would be going shopping for a very bright, pink shirt.

Later that afternoon when the girls and their father returned home, they sat Jackie down and informed her of the day's events. When Jas presented her arm for her mother's inspection, Jackie struggled to maintain an outwardly calm demeanor, as she inspected the arm not as a mother but as a highly trained registered nurse. She was immediately concerned regarding the size and scope of the injury, this did not represent what should have been perhaps an intense but small bruise, what she was observing encompassed most of Jasmine's upper arm.

SOLITARY TREE

Attempting to keep her voice from relaying a sudden onslaught of fear, she casually informed the girls that it was high time they went to their doctor for a physical exam.

CHAPTER FOURTEEN

"Hey Boss, you look tired today," casually remarked Herman Diaz as he sauntered into Mike's office and sat down, adding "Say Mike, when did you get so much gray hair? You have almost caught up to me!" teased Diaz, chuckling at his own lightly sardonic wit.

With his head still supported by the back of his chair and his eyes closed, Mike smiled informing Diaz that he was a fucking fountain of good news, and he sincerely appreciated the sharp observations of his deputy.

With the usual morning banter taken care of, Mike opened his eyes and the two of them quickly ran through the list of open case files and noted which one's seemed to be mired down.

Hearing the click of approaching heels on the linoleum floor in the outer office, Mike rose from his chair and completed his daily ritual by wishing Yolanda a good morning as she sat down at her desk.

"Good morning to you too," responded Yolanda displaying the broad smile that was so indicative of her personality.

During the past nine years that she has been Mike's secretary, there had been several times that Yolanda thought their relationship was on the verge of transcending that of secretary and boss, to something more substantial and intimate.

SOLITARY TREE

In the beginning, she had thought that her competition for
Mike's affection was Melody, the Forensic Pathologist from the
Medical Examiner's office, but in time she came to realize that
Mike's heart belonged to two small, lost girls.

Knowing that she could never compete with that, Yolanda
became involved in several relationships that had ended badly. In
her own words, she described them as abysmal failures, resulting
from the fact that her heart belonged to someone else. Resigning
herself to the fact that she may not ever have a place in Mike's
heart, being his secretary and getting to see him every day, along
with helping him navigate the myriad responsibilities of his
office will for the time being have to suffice.

Approximately one year ago, after watching a news program on
abducted children, Yolanda had suggested to Mike that he locate
an artist that would be able to create age enhanced portraits of
his daughters, from the pictures he had of them as young
children.

Exploiting his contacts with-in the Medical Examiner's office,
Mike obtained the services of an artist that they frequently turned
to in cold cases. After meeting with the artist and discussing
what he hoped to achieve, Mike reluctantly surrendered the
pictures he had of his girls just before they were abducted almost
ten years ago. The resultant portraits sent shock waves through
Mike's entire being, as he found himself staring at two beautiful
young ladies. It had taken the artist three months to complete,
but he was reasonably certain that the portraits would accurately
portray the girls if they were located tomorrow.

That evening before he sat down for dinner, Mike lovingly
placed the portraits of the girls on each of the place settings at
the kitchen table. Unable to tear his eyes away from the portraits,
Mike's grief over his loss is as great at this very moment, as it
was the day his girls were taken.

"Where are you?" Mike begged an answer from the two
beautiful, but mute girls who stared back at him from the
portraits.

CHAPTER FIFTEEN

The loud, abrasive knocking on his front door forcefully intruded into Mike's quiet reverie. Tearing his eyes away from his girl's portraits, he made his way to the door wondering who would be pounding on his door in this manner.

Opening the door, he saw the unmistakable form of Scarface seated on the front step with his back towards Mike.

As Mike moved forward and leaned against the wooden railing on his front porch he was surprised to see Scarface not dressed in the usual tuxedo. "What the hell are you doing sitting on my front porch!" demanded Mike.

"Ki wishes to see you," stated Scarface.

"Jesus! Don't you understand that I do not work for Ki, unlike yourself I am not one of his lackeys."

Ignoring the implied insult, Scarface simply replied that Mike needed to see Ki right away, it was a matter of life and death. Having said this, he then rose from his seated position and headed towards his parked car.

Cursing silently, Mike locked his house and followed Scarface in his own vehicle, wondering what the hell Scarface was referring to when he said it was a matter of life and death, Mike did not for a minute believe that Scarface had a flair for being melodramatic.

SOLITARY TREE

Aware of a nervous tick in his left cheek, causing minor muscle spasms, Mike rubbed it vigorously shaking off a twinge of fear that it might be his death Scarface had vaguely referred to.

Mike was shocked to see the difference in his Uncle, in the twelve months since Mike had last seen Ki, it looked like he had dropped fifty pounds and aged ten years, staring at this shrunken version of the old Ki Mike could almost, but not quite feel sorry for him. "You look like shit," Mike coldly informed Ki.
With Ki seated in his monolithic chair, Mike was forced to strain his hearing to perceive what his Uncle was saying. "Thank-you for that Mike, your empathy is truly touching, I'm only doing what every human at some point must do, and that is die. And like any other human the timing leaves something to be desired.

Apparently, I have an inoperable form of Brain Cancer, the good doctors have given me six months to get my affairs in order. So, I have commenced doing just that," taking a deep rasping breath, Ki then rattled off a string of Cantonese directed at Scarface and his brother.
The look of surprise on the face of Ki, and his body guards was priceless when Mike fired off his own round of Cantonese, informing the twins that if they wished to attempt to pluck hair from his head they were welcome to try, but they should also expect to get hurt in the process.
Staring at Mike with newfound respect, Ki nodded his head in approval at Mike's knowledge of the language. "You surprise Mike, I never thought to ask if you spoke Cantonese."
"My father taught me, it was all we spoke in our home, English was not allowed," Mike replied coldly.
Shaking his head in the negative Ki spoke quietly and succinctly. "That is impossible Mike, your father did not teach you to speak the language of our forefathers."
Shaking his head in exasperation at this statement by Ki, Mike asked him. "How in the fuck Ki, would you know what my father did or did not teach me," demanded an incredulous Mike, glaring at the wasted figure of Ki.

SOLITARY TREE

"For the simple reason that I, am your father," replied Ki.
This bombastic announcement by Ki, was greeted by Mike with
wholehearted scorn. Though it was undeniable that Mike bore a
strong physical resemblance to Ki, whereas Mike's father had
been a small framed, quiet, introspective individual who enjoyed
books and chess. Shaken though he was at this pronouncement
of Ki's, Mike laughed out loud in derision, coldly informing Ki
that the Brain Cancer had clearly ravaged his brain.
It was as though this reaction was exactly what Ki expected,
reaching into his shirt's breast pocket he removed a picture that
he waved in Mike's direction.
Stepping forward Mike impatiently grabbed the picture from
Ki's extended hand, and gazed upon an aged, crinkled, and
somewhat blurred Black and White photograph of three people.
Staring at the three people forever trapped with- in the
photograph, Mike was sure he recognized a much younger Ki,
there was also a tall, slim built, pretty, Caucasian lady with long
curly black hair, and standing between them holding their hands
was a young boy perhaps three years old gazing up at the lady.
As Mike continued to stare at the photo, Ki asked Mike how
many Asians did he know of that have curly hair. Ki explained in
detail the events that led up to Ki deciding that his brother should
raise Mike. When Mike was three years old his mother passed
away from a severe bout of pneumonia, Ki was caught up in a
gang war that he himself created, when he began to oust the
competition and seize control of the drug trade. Ki realizing that
he needed a safe place for his son to grow-up had approached his
younger brother Nickolas, with the idea that he would raise Ki's
son, and one day Mike would re-join his father at the head of the
empire that Ki had forged. Ki's brother Nick, was reluctant to
undertake this obligation until Ki informed him that he would be
well paid for his troubles, allowing him to stay at home and read
his be-loved books, and play chess.

SOLITARY TREE

What Ki had not counted on was his brother expounding ideals of law and order to his son, to the point where Mike sought a career in law enforcement. Several times over the last few years Ki had been ready to approach Mike, and inform him of his birth-right but it seemed there were always other, more urgent matters to attend to.

Staring at Ki in complete dis-belief at his spinning of this fairy tale, Mike regained his ability to speak.

"So, you expect me to believe that you are my father, that this woman in the picture is my mother, and that your brother and his wife raised me," shaking his head in sympathy Mike expressed his sincere belief that Ki was delusional. "Tell me this Ki, why after all these years would you want to suddenly claim me as your son?"

"The good doctors have instructed me to get my affairs in order. If you were to become the new leader of the empire I have created, it would mean the beginning of the Yee Dynasty. Now I wouldn't expect you to believe this story without benefit of medical science, therefore I had asked my assistants to extract two of your hairs with roots intact and submit it for DNA analysis. I have every confidence that it would prove beyond a doubt that I am your father."

"That is preposterous Ki!" Mike shouted scornfully. "You expect me to abandon every principle I have been taught, to become the quasi leader of a criminal organization. I have spent my entire adult life working sixty hours a week, to put assholes like you in jail where you belong. I find this demented scenario of yours to be not only repugnant, but morally reprehensible," avowed Mike, shaken to his very core by Ki's story. "If my father and mother were still alive, I'm sure they would immediately repudiate this bullshit story you're so desperately trying to sell," declared Mike vehemently. My father was a gentle, learned man, who believed in a society governed by laws. There is absolutely no way that he would condone your way of life, in fact he abhorred the very fact that you two were related."

SOLITARY TREE

"I won't argue that point with you Mike, I had often warned my brother that he was merely your shepherd, his obligation was to keep you safe until the time I re-claimed you. But, he mistakenly began to believe that you were his son, and espoused ideas to you that I forbid. I warned him and his wife many times to adhere to the original agreement, and to desist in attempting to alienate you from me. Unfortunately for them, they did not follow my explicit instructions, and therefore suffered the consequences for failing to do as ordered. Mike's face became ashen as the significance of Ki's words became clear. Experiencing a renewed sense of loss. Mike now realized that his parent's death was not caused by the actions of cowardly motorist, but rather by the cold-blooded psychopath seated in the chair facing him. "You had my parents killed!" bellowed Mike, boiling with rage by Ki's callous revelation.

  As though he were dealing with a slow-witted individual, Ki shook his head in frustration at Mike, and in a weak tired sounding voice that not long ago would have shook the walls asked Mike. "What are you failing to understand Mike? They were not your parents; they were your Aunt and Uncle. I am your Father, and your Mother passed away many years ago, as I said, if you choose not to believe me then we can have modern science settle the argument for us."

Staring at Ki with a mixture of horror, and cold fury Mike declared. "Never Ki! You will never be my father; all a DNA test might prove is that perhaps you were a sperm donor. Nothing more! A father is a person that shapes his children's lives, teaches them how to respect others, is there for them when they are sick, attends school functions, shares in their children's victories as if they were their own. You only have one interest, and that is you, the foundation of your so-called dynasty is based on the ruination of other people's lives." Taking a moment while he studied Ki seated in his ridiculous fucking chair, Mike continued in a voice that easily conveyed the disgust he felt for Ki.

SOLITARY TREE

"I'm finished here Ki. I wish you a slow, extremely painful death, that may, or may not allow you the chance to consider the grief you have caused others."

"Unfortunately, Mike, I was afraid you would have this very reaction, so I have taken steps that might convince you to think otherwise," displaying a wry smile directed at Mike, Ki remarked that since it would appear everyone here knew Cantonese, he acknowledged the fact that the element of surprise had been lost. Waving his hand at Scarface, Ki ordered him to approach and pass him the bag.

Watching Scarface approach Ki with a transparent white plastic bag, Mike could only wonder what Ki might be attempting now.

Extracting what looked like a small, hand held digital video recorder, Ki gestured weakly for Mike to take it.

"What's this Ki?", snorted Mike sarcastically. "Are these some touching family moments that you had recorded for posterity. Maybe a family Christmas dinner, or even better, one of my birthday's as a young boy."

"Just watch and you will see," whispered Ki.

Torn between his desire to leave Ki and everything that he represented, Mike succumbed to his curiosity and taking the recorder from Ki's weak grasp hit the play button.

The last thing that Mike expected to see was the re-playing of his execution style killing of O'Mallory, reaching the end of the short video clip, Mike raised his eyes towards Ki and growled. "What in the fuck is this Ki?"

"Unfortunately, Mike, you have forced my hand. I was afraid that you might be reluctant to accept your birthright, so when I arranged that little meeting with yourself and the unfortunate O'Mallory, I thought it prudent of me to capture it on film," excuse when I use your very own words. "For posterity sake, before you leave here Mike, you will have given me an answer. Either you will accept what I'm offering you, or that video will be the lead story on the late news tonight."

SOLITARY TREE

Staring at the loathsome, wasted figure of Ki, Mike began to chuckle which soon turned into loud boisterous laughter. "Do you realize how pathetic you are Ki?" enquired Mike with all traces of merriment absent from his voice. "You failed to convince me I'm your long-lost son, you failed miserably at attempting to lure me into your criminal organization, so now you stoop to blackmail. With father's like you who needs enemies," snorted Mike in disgust. "Oh ya, by the way Ki, the answer is still no."

Staring at Mike, Ki would not allow the grudging respect he felt for him, to be present either in his voice or his eyes. Ki was beginning to appreciate the fact that his brother had instilled a set of principles in Mike, that could not be bought or traded for. However, this would not sway his decision. "I'm disappointed that is your decision Mike, now you must live with the consequences. I have given you every opportunity to sit by my side, and inherit what I have created but since you so stubbornly refuse my offer, then I wish you good luck in explaining to your employer your actions captured in this video."

With a speed that caught Ki, and his body guards completely flatfooted, Mike drew his weapon from its holster, cocked it and pointed it squarely at Ki. "I think not Ki!" whispered Mike with deadly intent. Knowing that Ki himself posed no real threat, Mike turned his weapon to cover the bodyguards.

"I guess you failed to search him for weapons," enquired Ki looking with disgust at his body guards.

Shrugging his shoulders in helpless resignation, Scarface admitted to his boss that they had forgotten to.

"Well Mike, what do we do now?" enquired Ki with a slight smirk. "It would appear that you temporarily have the upper hand due to my employee's lax work ethic. But, rest assured you will not leave this building alive," pointing towards Scarface's twin brother, Ki informed Mike that Shawn had likely already deployed the locking mechanism on the outer door.

SOLITARY TREE

"In answer to your question Ki, this is what we're going to do," commented Mike displaying no outward emotion at Ki's threat. Speaking rapidly in Cantonese, Mike asked the twins a question. Taking a minute before answering, Shawn then fired back a reply in the sing song dialect of Cantonese. The look of shock that registered on Ki's face was one of outrage and dis-belief.

Acting on Shawn's verbal warning, Mike turned swiftly on the balls of his feet to face Ki, who was in the act of withdrawing a gun from a cleverly hidden pocket, sewn into the side of his chair.

Snarling at Shawn for his treasonous warning, Ki continued to pull the weapon from its hiding place, and placed it on his lap. "What are you going to do Mike, shoot me?" asked Ki.

"Now that you mention it Ki, yes, I am," responded Mike casually. The sudden, ripping, thunderclap explosions that roared from Mike's gun assaulted the ears of Mike and the twins. Ki however never heard the explosions, as he was dead before his head slammed into the back of the chair driven there by the force of the two sub-sonic missiles from Mike's gun. The trio watched dispassionately as Ki's body slowly slid from the chair, and became a puddle of human detritus in front of the chair Ki had been so proud of.

Watching the twins with the highest degree of vigilance, Mike asked Shawn. "Why did you warn me?"

"Ki was no longer strong enough to run the organization, there have already been threats from people who, while Ki was healthy were afraid of their own mothers," studying Ki's corpse, Shawn shrugged his shoulders and admitted that Mike had just saved them the trouble of executing Ki themselves.

"What happens now," Mike asked the brothers

"That's up to you Mike," answered a reflective sounding Shawn. "If you choose to leave here and never look back that's fine, if you decide that you want to take Ki's place, then we might have a problem."

SOLITARY TREE

Pointing in the direction of the discarded video camera lying on the floor, Mike asked them if there were any copies made of the tape contained within.

At this juncture, Scarface moved to the far wall in the room, pushing a small, hidden button a section of the faux wood paneling slid noiselessly away, revealing a small safe.

Entering a short sequence of numbers, Mike heard an audible click as the safe opened, revealing numerous contents with-in. Extracting a small bag, Scarface studied it for a minute before returning to his brother and Mike.

"This is the only copy that was made Mike. I know because I made it," Scarface assured him as he extended the bag towards Mike. Accepting the bag, Mike moved towards the video camera and took possession of it as well. "Who took the video?" queried Mike.

"Not to worry Mike," responded Shawn. "Twenty-four hours after the incident, Ki had the guy who shot the video killed."

Mike was not at all surprised by this dispassionate comment of Shawn's, it seemed Ki had a penchant for ordering people killed.

Pointing towards Ki, Mike asked the twins what will become of the body.

"It will never be discovered," Shawn assured Mike.

"I wasn't here!" declared Mike as he made his way towards the exit, without so much as a second look at the very dead Ki.

"We don't even fuckin know you," replied the twin's in unison.

With his mind in a blur over the events that had transpired in the last two hours, Mike found himself sitting alone in a booth, in a nameless bar, with eight empty shot glasses forming a pyramid in front of him. Reaching into his pocket Mike removed his cell phone and placed a call. "Herman? Ya it's Mike. Hey listen I'm, just a second," leaning slightly out of the booth Mike yelled at the bartender asking him the name of the fuckin bar.

"It's Mike's Bar and Grill," yelled the Bartender.

"You're shittin me, right?" Mike yelled back at the Bartender.

SOLITARY TREE

"Nope! No shit buddy, you're at Mike's Bar and Grill on forty-second Street."

"You gotta be fucking kidding me," chortled Mike as he relayed the information to Diaz. Mike then asked Herman if he would be able to pick him up in two hours as he planned on getting seriously drunk.

CHAPTER SIXTEEN

Awaiting the arrival of their family physician Johnathan Daniels who had requested this meeting, Jackie and Barry were mildly apprehensive. It had been two weeks since their daughter's annual physical checkups, ordinarily they would receive a card with a happy face advising them the girls were in excellent health, this time however they had been invited to meet with their doctor to discuss those very physicals. Jackie had first met Johnathan Andrews many years ago, when he began his internship at the hospital where Jackie was a registered nurse, they had struck an instant rapport and as soon as Johnathan could begin his own practice, Jackie and Barry became his first patients.

In his early fifties, Johnathan was the epitome of a kind and caring physician, with his soft voice and gentle manners, the tall, thin, slightly stooped figure, with an unruly mop of gray hair was in high demand. His busy office receptionist was forced to explain to hopeful parents, that unfortunately Johnathan was unable to accept any more patients.

Jackie and Barry attempted to keep their nameless fear at bay by conversing about the upcoming school graduation, knowing that in a few short years it will be their daughters turn to achieve that milestone. Hearing Johnathan's office door open Barry and Jackie simultaneously looked over their shoulder as the harried looking Johnathan entered and wished them good morning. Apologizing for his tardiness, Johnathan explained that he had an emergency at the hospital that had required his attention.

SOLITARY TREE

Taking a moment to shuffle some files to the far side of his desk, Johnathan cleared his throat before speaking.

"Now, I don't want to be an alarmist, but, during the routine testing of the girl's blood samples, it seemed that one of them came back testing positive for Kidney disease, I immediately requested a second test to affirm the findings.

Unfortunately, the second test did just that, I was hoping that there was an error in the lab's findings. I would like to ask the both of you to think if Jas had complained lately of her ankles or feet swelling, or has she seemed unusually tired?"

Taking a moment to ponder his question, Jackie did voice some concerns that Jas seemed to be tired a lot lately, and the other day when she had Jas help her move some furniture around, she seemed to be short of breath. At the time, Jackie had thought maybe it was merely due to seasonal allergies.

"What I would like to do is have Jas come in for another set of blood tests." Gazing at the shocked couple seated across his desk from him, Johnathan stood up moved around his desk and plucking an unused chair from the small coffee table, placed it beside the couple and sat down. He explained to them that labs have been known to make errors, sometimes they get samples and patients mixed up, I don't want to raise any false hopes, but to err on the side of caution I would like to have Jas come in and we will do some additional blood work."

Unable to control his anxiety, Barry launched himself from his chair, and began to pace the room. "So, you're saying that Jas has a Kidney disease" probed an apprehensive Barry.

Attempting to placate Barry's elevated level of anxiety, Johnathan calmly re-iterated the fact that until he was completely satisfied the lab did not err, then no, he is not convinced that Jas is indeed testing positive for Acute Kidney failure. Johnathan went on to explain to the worried parents that there are a host of other symptoms associated with this disease, and that as far as he could tell Jas was not displaying any of those.

SOLITARY TREE

"In conclusion, I refuse to accept the worst-case scenario based on one set of tests, if the next set of blood work tests positive, at that time we will map out our strategy to combat this illness. Having said that, I would like both the girls in here as soon as possible to draw the sample and have the lab expedite their analysis, so that we have a definitive answer in a couple of days."

At this point, Jackie questioned Johnathan about the need to have both the girls provide new samples.

With a small smile, Johnathan explained that it would likely spare Jas some angst, if both girls were asked, rather than Jas alone.

Fully appreciating Johnathan's thoughtfulness, Jackie informed him that the girls will be here immediately after school.

Still feeling highly agitated, Barry and Jackie thanked Johnathan knowing that their doctor had the girl's best interests at heart.

Leaving the doctor's office, both parents were in a state of shock still attempting to come to grips with the reality that their daughter's precious life might be at risk. "We can only hope for the best Barry," stated Jackie as she witnessed a single tear escape from her husband's eye.

Wiping away the tear with his hand Barry, echoed Jackie's optimistic statement.

The girls were a little surprised to see their Mom waiting for them in front of the school that afternoon, usually the girls would walk the short distance home. Both Jas, and Sandy groaned out loud when their Mom informed them that the blood samples they had given at the time of their physicals had been misplaced.

"That sucks!" complained Sandy. "I hate when they stick that needle in me and watch the blood fill the syringe. It's gross," she concluded.

Jas was a little more phlegmatic, telling her sister that it only takes a minute and it's not like it hurts.

SOLITARY TREE

Driving the short distance to their doctor's office, Jasmine informed her Mom that she must be retaining water, because the elastic in her socks have left rings on her ankles. Jackie was hard pressed to maintain her outward composure, knowing full well that these might be indicators of the other symptoms that Johnathan had vaguely referred to.

With the bloodwork completed and sent off to the lab, Jackie and the girls headed home, the girls had time to change and tackle their homework, while Barry and Jackie had a glass of wine before the spaghetti dinner that Barry had prepared, would be ready.

With the girls safely ensconced in their respective rooms doing their homework for school, Barry and Jackie had a chance to quietly discuss their fears. Jackie decided not to inform Barry of the information that Jas had disclosed that afternoon.

Knowing full well that Jas may be facing the toughest battle of her young life, Barry and Jackie made a solemn promise to each other that they would never allow Jas to see their fear.

CHAPTER SEVENTEEN

As news of Ki's murder resonated through both the law enforcement community, and like-wise the criminal one, it was widely feared that a deadly turf war would be initiated by the small-time criminals that Ki had held at bay for so long through fear of swift and brutal retribution. Their fears proved to be groundless, it quickly became apparent that Ki's murder was in fact, orchestrated by his very own body guards, the successful coup had now left them in charge of Ki's empire and were rapidly proving to be every bit as ruthless as Ki.

Suffering from what had to be worst hang over he had ever endured, Mike opened his desk drawer and shook two aspirins from the half empty bottle, then washed them down with several mouthfuls of water. Knowing that he could have easily begged off today and stayed home to suffer through this torment, didn't help. When Herman Diaz had rescued him from of all places, Mike's Bar and Grill the night before, Diaz had joked with Mike stating. "Bet you won't make it into the office tomorrow."

Mike was sure he had a ten-dollar bill riding on that bet, at least he hoped he did, otherwise he would much prefer to be home. Shaking his head, he once again forced his eyes to focus on the report he was reading concerning the now deceased Ki.

Rubbing his temples in a futile effort to ease the pounding, Mike closed his eyes and did some serious soul searching. Knowing that not only had Ki killed his beloved parents, Ki was also directly responsible for many other people's deaths, did that justify Mike's killing him?

SOLITARY TREE

Or was Ki right when he declared himself to be Mike's father, and Mike's actions simply reflected those of the man he hated. An ordered society would certainly not condone his actions, but in retrospect, Ki did not exist in an ordered society, his was a world of tooth and claw, where indecisive action would be interpreted as weakness.

Not hearing any movement betraying the fact that someone had entered his office, Mike was surprised when he heard Diaz laugh out loud and exclaim. "Jesus Mike, you look like shit! How's the head feeling their big guy?" Diaz laughed uproariously as Mike displayed a hand with a raised middle finger.

"Jesus Diaz, keep it down to a dull roar would you! There's people suffering here. Hey, by the way I think you owe me ten bucks," commented Mike, finally opening his eyes.

"Worth every penny seeing you suffer like this," replied Diaz with a smile broad enough to break cheek muscles.

Smiling as he plucked the ten-dollar bill from Diaz's hand, Mike displayed a superhuman effort in not submitting to the waves of nausea that were crashing repeatedly in his stomach.

Watching his boss closely, Diaz suggested to Mike that closing his door and stretching out on the office couch for a short while might have some merit.

Snapping his fingers, Diaz commented. "Say Mike, do you happen to remember that low level drug dealer named Curly?"

Watching Diaz through bloodshot eyes, Mike grunted something that sounded like an affirmative.

"Yes, well seems he has turned up dead, and it would appear that he did not die easy. Someone decided that they were carvers, and used Curly's chest as their block of wood when they carved the word rat."

This information caused Mike to brush aside his temporary misery while he questioned Diaz further. "When did this occur? I have yet to see any reports."

SOLITARY TREE

"An informant that I use, was telling me that as of right now Curly is in the Medical Examiner's freezer waiting to be identified."

"Shit!" murmured Mike as the events of almost a decade ago came roaring back. "That's the guy who gave up Larry Donovan, he was hoping to cut a deal with the District Attorney's office when he was arrested for the third time selling drugs.

He knew he was facing some serious time and thought he could make a trade. I had heard the District Attorney had him placed in witness protection where he would hopefully survive until it all went to trial, but it never made it to the courtroom as they have been unable to capture Donovan."

"Looks like maybe your old partner caught up to him," mused Diaz thoughtfully.

"Well if he had been in witness protection, he sure as fuck wouldn't have been in the City, so he must have decided that he was safe from Donovan and vacated the program," voiced Mike as he contemplated the death of Curly and its possible ramifications. "You know what Herman, one Sunday night I thought that I caught a glimpse of Donovan on the street in front of my house, but the guy had disappeared by the time I got there."

"Jesus Christ Mike! Do you think he was going to make a move on you?" questioned Diaz.

"Hard to say, the last time he contacted me I swore I was going to shoot first and ask questions later," adding with a wry smile. "So, I'm pretty sure he's not my friend. But now that I think of it that was quite a while ago, so who knows what the asshole had in mind."

Deciding to change the subject Diaz asked Mike. "I hope you don't mind me asking Mike, but the wife and I were talking last night after I delivered you home safe and sound, how long has it been since your girls were taken?"

"Ten years on the tenth of May," Mike responded soberly.

SOLITARY TREE

Shaking his head in wonder that so many years, had elapsed so rapidly, Diaz excused himself leaving Mike to suffer through his hangover.

Cradling his pounding head in intertwined fingers, Mike once again pondered why thus far, his life had been so fucked up.

Deciding that the tapping he was hearing was someone knocking discreetly on his office door, and not directly related to what was going on in his head, Mike advised whoever was pounding on his door to please desist, warning them that unless they wished to see him vomit they had best leave.

Raising his head when his door opened, Mike was not at all surprised to see his assistant Yolanda enter carting a green garbage can.

Unable to decide if he was annoyed, or amused, Mike pointed at the garbage can and asked her. "What the hell is that for?"

"You said you were about to vomit, well then vomit in this please, as you don't pay me enough to clean up your mess," declared an irate Yolanda adding sarcastically. "Don't think for a minute that I'm about to hold your hand while you vomit."

Despite the misery he was feeling, Mike smiled at her sharp-tongued tirade, gazing at her through bloodshot eyes, Mike realized that in the ten years they have worked together, Yolanda still possessed the same lithe figure she had when she began working for Mike. She had for the last few years allowed her hair to grow, and it now cascaded to her shoulders, surprising both himself and Yolanda, Mike asked her if she would like to have supper that night.

"Mike, I have supper every night," Yolanda responded smartly.

"I'm sorry, I meant would you like to have supper with me," clarified Mike.

Not wanting to let him off the hook too easily, Yolanda busied herself arranging files on his desk before announcing that he could pick her up at seven pm, and that she expected him to be wearing a tie.

SOLITARY TREE

Returning to her desk, Yolanda was pleasantly surprised with this unexpected dinner invitation, during her tenure, as Mike's assistant Yolanda has had several relationships.
She even married one of her suitors, but it was an abysmal failure, barely a year into the marriage both parties concluded that they had married for all the wrong reasons. With the insight gained from that ghastly foray into wedded bliss, she had immersed herself in her work, knowing that the life partner she sought was emotionally crippled and may never be obtainable.
Unsure why he was feeling inordinately anxious regarding his dinner date with Yolanda, Mike took one last look in the bathroom vanity mirror. The reflection in the mirror revealed a moderately attractive man in his early forties, his gray curly hair was slightly longer then was thought to be fashionable, the vertical lines etched on his face were testament to the fact that his life had not been without adversity.
Wearing his favorite gray slacks, with the slightly darker shirt and tie, Mike knocked on Yolanda's door at precisely seven p.m.
Hearing Yolanda's voice from with-in the apartment advising him the door was open Mike let himself in. He was not prepared for what happened next as Yolanda walked through the tiny kitchen towards him, it was as though he had never seen the true beauty that she exuded. If he had to describe it, he would have called it an aura, an ethereal quality that Mike had somehow never before perceived.
Approaching Mike wearing a simple dress whose color was reminiscent of ripe peaches, Yolanda turned her back to Mike and as though it were a ritual they had practiced many times, she requested that he do up the zipper on the dress.
With fingers that seemed to have suddenly transformed into thumbs, Mike struggled briefly with the zipper before it relented and allowed Mike to bridge the gap, and once again conceal the lightly tanned skin of Yolanda's back.

SOLITARY TREE

The evening was an unmitigated success, it seemed that even though they had known each other, and worked closely together for ten years, it felt like they had finally become aware of each other. Their conversation during dinner, was the conduit that allowed them insight into waters that had thus far never been chartered. It was only when they were advised by their waiter that the restaurant was closing, did they realize that four hours had sped by.

The next morning Mike arose and prepared a light breakfast which he delivered to the still drowsy Yolanda. Watching her as she sat up in bed, placing a pillow on her lap to set the breakfast laden tray on, Mike felt a sense of contentment that had eluded him for the last decade.

CHAPTER EIGHTEEN

Waiting for Barry and Jackie Wentworth in his office, Dr. Johnathan Andrews loathed this part of being a health care professional, it was never easy informing people that their loved ones were seriously ill.

Rising from his seated position behind his desk, Johnathan moved to welcome Jackie and Barry as his receptionist ushered them into his office.

After seating the two concerned looking parents, Johnathan once again took his seat behind the desk. Opening the file which contained the newest results of Jas's blood work, and even though he had the results memorized he still took a minute to re-read the information contained with-in. Taking a deep breath, he slowly began to speak. "I sincerely wish there was an easy way to tell you folks this. The results of Jasmine's blood work have arrived; I am so sorry to say that she has tested positive for Acute Kidney Failure." Johnathan watched in sorrow as expressions of shock, fear, closely followed by desperation crossed the faces of not only the people who were his patients but also his friends.

"Jesus Christ!" exclaimed Barry. "What do we do now?"

"I will admit Jasmine to the hospital immediately as there are some further tests that need to be done," stated Johnathan. "We will need to ascertain the rate her kidneys are functioning at to determine the level of Potassium present in her bloodstream. Unfortunately, kidney disease is not always restricted primarily to the kidneys, it may result in damage to the heart, as well the central nervous system."

SOLITARY TREE

   With an expression that clearly displayed the compassion he felt for Barry and Jackie, Johnathan informed them the hospital was expecting Jasmine, and the admitting paperwork had been filed. For the time being there was no need to have Jasmine placed in the Intensive Care Unit, so he had her booked into a private room.

"We will have Jasmine there in half an hour," announced Jackie.

   As promised Barry and Jackie delivered a worried Jasmine to the hospital with-in thirty minutes. Although they did their best to downplay the seriousness of the situation, Jasmine knew that she was seriously ill as she had not been feeling well for quite a while, not wanting to inform her parents in the hope that she would get over whatever it was she had.

   With the nurses bustling about getting Jasmine comfortable in the hospital bed and hooked up to the various monitors, they attempted to keep Jasmine's mood upbeat enquiring about her boyfriends and school.

   While that was taking place, Johnathan met briefly with Barry and Jackie, hoping that when they realized he had a definite strategy in place it might help to lessen their degree of anxiety.

   "I will have a cot placed in the room as well," advised Johnathan. "I know that if Jasmine were my daughter I would not wish to see her spending the nights alone in the hospital."

   Thanking Johnathan for his thoughtfulness Barry and Jackie left the patient interview room and joined their daughter.

CHAPTER NINETEEN

"Where would you like this Yolanda?" gasped a sweating
Herman Diaz as he struggled with the last box laden with books.
Quickly scanning the contents of the box, she informed him that
it could go downstairs, then advised Herman that there is Pizza
and Beer in the kitchen.
Standing randomly around the kitchen eating Pizza, and sipping
cold Beer, the five close friends that had assisted Yolanda and
Mike in the move, were joking about whose back was hurting the
most.
Shortly thereafter, when their help had departed Mike and
Yolanda carried their cold drinks out to the deck and relaxed,
chuckling to themselves about some of the antics their friends
had committed that morning.
Turning serious, Yolanda informed Mike that she did not want
to get married.
"Oh, I see," laughed Mike. "You will move in with me, but
won't marry me."
"No I won't," declared Yolanda. "I have already initiated the
legal process to change my last name to Chance. I'm not about to
allow a shitty little piece of paper interfere with what we have
now. We have finally found each other; we both love and respect
each other, as far as I'm concerned we do not need to have some
stranger tell us what to do, or how to treat each other."
Staring at Yolanda while she explained this to him, Mike asked
her one simple question. "Are you happy?"

SOLITARY TREE

Returning the stare, Yolanda lovingly informed Mike that there were not enough adjectives to describe what she is feeling. "Happy does not begin to do justice to what I'm feeling!" reaching across the short distance that separated them she grasped his hand and spoke softly declaring. "Michael Chance, it has taken a decade for us to realize that what we sought was right in front of us. For us the journey starts here and now! It has been two months now since we found each other, I cannot begin to describe how contented I am. We will never stop searching for our daughters, the only thing that could possibly make me happier is the day our girls are seated at the kitchen table with us."

As Mike listened attentively to Yolanda, he wondered how one simple dinner date had culminated in her now living with him. Hearing her refer to his daughters as her own, caused small tears of joy to escape from his eyes.

CHAPTER TWENTY

Closing the door on his personal vehicle, Mike heard someone call his name, looking around the parking lot at the precinct Mike spotted Diaz waving at him. Smiling as his out of breath Deputy caught up to him, Mike slapped him on the back laughing as he stated that maybe Diaz should consider losing some weight.

Still in the process of catching his breath, Diaz grunted something to the effect that Mike could go fuck himself. Laughing out loud at this, Mike patiently waited for his good friend to catch his breath.

Slowly making their way towards the precinct building, Herman advised Mike that he had something he would like to run by Mike if he had time today.

"I know I have to meet with the budget committee this morning, maybe check with Yolanda I'm sure she will be able to squeeze you in to my busy schedule."

"Busy! That's funny Mike, everyone knows you senior managers play golf all day, every day," guffawed Diaz.

Entering the precinct through the revolving doors, Mike waved farewell to Diaz as he headed off to his meeting.

It wasn't until later that afternoon that Mike met with Diaz. With the two friends seated in Mike's office, Diaz sprung his idea on Mike. "Every year the Angela and I go to Vernon, British Columbia, in Canada for our vacation, unfortunately with her declining health we have decided that maybe this year we will stay home. Since we have a long-standing reservation at a small resort on the lake there, she suggested that maybe Yolanda and yourself would like to go in our stead."

SOLITARY TREE

"I'm sorry to hear that Angela is not doing well," commiserated Mike.

"Thanks for that Mike, her arthritis does seem to be worsening." Punching the often-used number on his phone that connected him to Yolanda's phone, he asked her if she had a minute to come into his office. Mike never tired of watching Yolanda slip so effortlessly into his office, her style of walking was unique unto herself, once Yolanda was seated, Mike invited Herman to explain to Yolanda his idea.

As Herman began speaking about the city of Vernon, situated at the north end of the Okanagan Valley Lake, in British Columbia, Canada, his fondness for the area was clearly evident in his voice. Herman spent the next thirty minutes extolling the virtues of the area so eloquently, that his enraptured audience began to feel they were already there, from sagebrush covered grasslands, dotted with half-wild cattle and horses, to heavily forested mountains. He explained in detail the robust wine industry located in the Valley, the numerous Estate Winery's that in a very short time have produced world class vintages. "The only reason Angela and myself have not re-located there is because the snow, and cold temperatures in the winter would make Angela's arthritis unbearable," concluded Herman regretfully.

"What do you think?" queried Mike.

"I think it's absolutely wonderful Herman, it's so generous of Angela and yourself to offer it to us," exclaimed an excited Yolanda.

Beaming with pleasure that they had accepted his offer, Herman gave them a brochure on the resort, and informed them of the week the reservation was made for.

That night, Mike and Yolanda checked to ensure their respective passports were still current, since they would be needed to enter Canada. Allowing themselves three days to drive to the resort, Mike and Yolanda felt like they were on a honeymoon.

SOLITARY TREE

They stopped at out of the way places to enjoy a picnic lunch, one day they spent three idyllic hours walking along a grassy trail that paralleled a slow-moving meandering stream, and were rewarded when they encountered a large brown bear cavorting in the water. They weren't sure if he was attempting to catch fish, or just having fun in the middle of the stream on a hot day, either way he provided a form of entertainment for Mike and Yolanda, that would have them telling all their friends back home. Eventually they found their way to the resort and were immediately struck by its natural beauty, parking their car at the office, Mike attended to the checking in procedures, then with cabin key in hand, hopped back in the vehicle to go in search of their cabin. Entering the rustic one bedroom cabin Mike and Yolanda were instantly in love with its simplicity, there was even a stainless-steel gallon bucket in which to carry water from the old-fashioned pump located a couple of hundred feet away from the cabin.

Laughing like two care-free teenagers, Mike and Yolanda quickly transferred their clothes and camping articles from their car into the cabin.

Grabbing the empty water pail, Yolanda handed it to Mike and sporting a huge smile asked him to. "Please fetch us some water, kind sir."

"Gladly," exclaimed Mike taking ownership of the pail then whistling softly headed down the trail towards the water pump.

It was on his way to the water pump that Mike became instantly immobile, releasing the bucket he never heard the clang it made as it bounced off a small rock. Swearing under his breath at what he was observing, words long thought forgotten returned with a resounding crash in his mind. Closing his eyes, he re-opened them to the same vista, standing there before him was a flag-pole, suspended from that pole was the Canadian flag, the Maple Leaf.

SOLITARY TREE

In the background, the Emerald hued Kal Lake, the words the fortune teller Gwendolyn, spoke almost a decade ago were once again remembered as though it were only yesterday.

"The girls are alive, I see a Solitary Tree, bearing a Single Leaf, with a large body of water."

Rushing back towards the cabin, Mike called to Yolanda to come outside. Detecting a peculiar quality in Mike's voice, Yolanda swiftly left the cabin, meeting Mike on the trail.

With a smile that stretched from ear to ear, Mike excitedly informed her that he had something to show her. Quickly returning to the spot, Mike asked Yolanda if she remembered the time when acting on a whim he had decided to see a fortune teller.

Not knowing where Mike was going with this, Yolanda informed Mike that she vaguely remembered him mentioning that.

Gently turning Yolanda so that she was looking exactly where Mike had just happened to look, he softly recited Gwendolyn's words into her ear.

"Jesus Christ Mike!" exclaimed Yolanda breathlessly. "Could it be possible? How else could she have known these things, unless she actually saw our daughters here."

With tears flowing freely down his cheeks, Mike was ecstatic, after all these long years, this was the first tangible evidence that perhaps their daughters were alive.

If anyone at that time would have happened along the trail, they would have been puzzled and perhaps even alarmed as they witnessed two people clinging together, with tears streaming down their faces.

Making their way back to the cabin still minus the water pail, Mike plucked two cold beers form the ice filled cooler, then wiping away their residual tears with a Kleenex, they began to brainstorm.

SOLITARY TREE

"I don't want to be the devil's advocate Mike, but this is a very large area, and we are basing our hopes on the word of a fortune teller," stated a cautiously optimistic Yolanda.

Taking a long slow drink, Mike closed his eyes and contemplated their next move, then giving voice to what he hoped might be a reasonable plan of action, informed Yolanda.

"You're absolutely right Yolanda, this is a large area and we are basing our hopes on the word of a fortune teller. After almost ten long years with absolutely no clue as to their whereabouts, we will leave no stone unturned. I think what we should do is head to the local police station, we should then contact Diaz and have him go to the house and fax the girl's pictures to the cops. I just hope we are able to accomplish that before they have us committed as people suffering from severe delusional issues," concluded Mike with a rueful smile. "Once we have the pictures, the local cops just might recognize them. I realize that at best it's a weak plan, but right now it's our only plan."

Nodding her head in agreement at Mike's suggestion, Yolanda voiced her opinion that any plan is better than no plan.

With the vacation temporarily put on hold, Mike and Yolanda hopped back into their vehicle, and were about to proceed to the local Police station when Yolanda asked Mike if by chance he might know where it was at.

Staring across the seat at Yolanda, Mike laughed and reminded her that she's the administrator, he just assumed she would know these things.

Taking a minute to formulate a plan of her own, Yolanda suggested that Mike stop at the resort's office, where she will enquire as to the whereabouts of the local Police Office.

Following Yolanda's sage advice, Mike stopped at the Resort's office and Yolanda exited the car with the hopes of securing the needed information. Mike was immediately alarmed when Yolanda returned to the car in less than a minute, her normally healthy tanned face had been replaced with a ghostly pallor.

Staring out the vehicle's windshield as though stupefied, Yolanda began to speak slowly and succinctly.

SOLITARY TREE

"Michael!" she exclaimed. "Who was working in the office when you checked us in?"

Alarmed at this transformation in Yolanda, thinking that in the ten years he had known Yolanda she had never once addressed him as Michael.

Mike thought about it for a minute then answered. "Young kid, maybe seventeen, heavyset, had gold, wire framed glasses, I believe they were oval. He was very friendly, picked up on my accent right away. Why?" asked Mike, concerned by this sudden change in Yolanda.

Taking a deep breath, Yolanda informed Mike that the kid he described was no longer working in the office. "There is an incredibly beautiful young lady working in the office Mike, and as I live and breathe I swear its Desiree," murmured Yolanda.

Feeling his heart hammer against his ribs, Mike quietly asked Yolanda to please repeat what she had said. Hearing it a second time caused Mike's hand to become instantly slick with moisture, staring out the windshield, he mechanically wiped his hands dry on his jeans.

Turning to face Mike, with tears of joy coursing down her face, Yolanda once again informed Mike that she had just talked to Desiree.

As a Tsunami of emotions flooded his being, he dimly heard Yolanda ask why he's not going in to see their daughter.

"I'm fuckin scared Yolanda.!" blurted Mike. "After all this time what if it's not her. I have finally reached a point in my life where I'm happy, I have the woman I love sitting next to me, I have almost accepted the fact that we may never see our daughters again. Do you really think it's her?" queried Mike desperately seeking confirmation.

"Michael," soothed Yolanda. "That beautiful young Asian girl in that office, can be none other than Desiree Chance. Now you need to unbuckle your seatbelt and go in and talk to our daughter."

As though in a daze, Mike followed Yolanda's advice.

SOLITARY TREE

With his heart hammering against his chest wall to the point he thought he was about to have a heart attack, Mike pushed the office door open and entered the building.

Exercising every ounce of self-control at his disposal, Mike was barely able to project the façade of a polite, and somewhat curious tourist while having a conversation with the attractive young Asian girl who was now working in the office. Mike intuitively knew the minute he set eyes on the young lady that it could be none other than Desiree. Attempting to glean any information, Mike introduced himself, mentioning that he was a Police Officer from the United States. He was rewarded when the young lady countered with her own name, Mike casually remarked that when he had checked in there was a young man that looked after him, the young lady informed Mike that her cousin Raymond had to leave, and had asked her if she would cover for him. Feigning interest in the brochures that promoted local points of interest, Mike casually asked the young lady how long she had lived in the area, Mike was immediately crestfallen when she informed him that she had lived here all her life, he then asked some gently probing questions regarding possible siblings, and if they also worked here at the resort. Recognizing the body language exuded by the young lady, Mike knew that he was fast approaching the line between curious tourist, and invading private space, not wishing to alienate the young lady Mike thanked her profusely for her time and left.

Hopping into his vehicle, Mike quickly started it and with Yolanda staring at him, found his way out of the resort and headed down Kal Lake road towards town. After proceeding half a Kilometer, Mike found a wide spot on the shoulder of the road that would allow him to safely pull the car over.

SOLITARY TREE

Once the vehicle was parked and turned off, Mike turned to face
Yolanda, and with a smile that initiated in his heart, and
climaxed on his lips, announced to Yolanda that although the
young girl introduced herself as Sandie Wentworth, he's positive
she's Desiree.

At a loss to accurately convey what he's feeling, Mike removed
himself from the vehicle and began to restlessly pace back and
forth on the narrow path that ran parallel to the road.

Joining Mike on the side of the road, Yolanda had to step
directly in front of him forcing him to stop his pacing.

"What's the matter Mike?" questioned Yolanda.

"I'm not sure Yolanda," replied a deeply shaken Mike. "When
the girls were abducted, I never thought it would take a decade to
find them. Now, by the purest stroke of luck you found Desiree,
what do we do? Let's assume the girls are still together, and live
here with a family. Do we, after a decade of separation have the
right to intrude in their lives?" leaning against the car and
rubbing his face with his hands as though to clear away cobwebs
Mike looked searchingly at Yolanda for an answer.

"Michael Chance!" scolded an angry Yolanda. "You, more than
anyone have that right. You are their biological father; these
children were stolen from you, then sold to the Jacob's in
Florida. How do you know they weren't also sold to whoever
they live with now? For now, we will assume that both girls are
together, so we must decide how best we go about informing the
local police that a crime may have been perpetrated. If nothing
else the girls deserve to know the truth, who knows what they
have been told about you, maybe they were told that you and
Adele abandoned them."

Gazing at Yolanda, Mike asked her softly. "Why did it take me
ten years to realize that what I was looking for, was right in front
of me?"

CHAPTER TWENTY-ONE

Entering the medium sized building that housed the local detachment of the Royal Canadian Mounted Police, Mike and Yolanda crossed the room to where a younger looking Police Officer was leafing through some posters.

Raising his head, he acknowledged their presence, then asked them to please wait as he was just about finished.

Placing the posters on a shelf below the level of the countertop, the young R.C.M.P. officer apologized for the delay and enquired as to how he could be of assistance.

Introducing himself and Yolanda, Mike presented his Metro-City Chief of Detectives Identification to the young officer.

Nodding his head as he scanned Mike's identification, stating. "Don't ask me!"

A surprised Mike and Yolanda stared at the cop, wondering what the hell he was talking about.

Smiling, the cop advised them that it seemed most American cops liked to ask where the R.C.M.P. kept their horses.

Shrugging his shoulders in puzzlement at this statement, Mike admitted that the thought had never crossed his mind.

"Oh, by the way I'm auxiliary constable Roland Perkins, so what can I do for you folks?"

"Do you happen to have a private interview room that we could use?" demanded an impatient Yolanda, already wearied of Perkin's lack of professionalism.

SOLITARY TREE

"Yes, I believe we have a room available," motioning for Mike and Yolanda to walk around the end of the counter.

Following Perkins down a narrow hallway, Mike unobtrusively counted no less than twelve cops, he was surprised at this large number, knowing that this might represent only the afternoon shift.

Ushering Mike and Yolanda into the vacant eight- foot by ten-foot interview room, Perkins invited them to make themselves comfortable while he located someone to talk to.

Observing the stark furnishings in the windowless room, Mike chuckled, commenting to Yolanda that the RCMP must have identical budgetary constraints as the cops back home did. Pulling out two hard backed wooden chairs from the single folding table, they sat down hoping that it would not be a long wait.

Although barely ten minutes had elapsed since they had entered the room, it seemed like an hour sitting on those horrible chairs, in fact Yolanda had risen from hers informing Mike she would rather stand. Suddenly the door opened allowing a middle aged, average sized gentleman to enter, who introduced himself as Staff Sergeant Bruce Hanley. Indicating Mike with a nod of his head, he mentioned that it was always nice to meet a cop from another jurisdiction. Taking a seat, Bruce smiled as he apologized for the god-awful chairs, admitting that he was sure they were designed to persuade criminals to confess so they can get the hell out of them.

Seated across the table from Mike and Yolanda with his writing tablet placed on the table, Bruce glanced at his watch making a note that the interview began at eighteen- hundred.

"I guess it's safe to assume that you did not request this audience to protest a parking ticket," queried Bruce, bestowing a warm smile upon Mike and Yolanda.

SOLITARY TREE

Mike instinctively knew that although Bruce may be exuding a friendly persona, cops everywhere are cut from the same bolt of cynical material, daily forced to deal with habitual liars this can at times prove to be an impediment when they do hear the truth. Understanding this mentality, Mike slowly began to communicate to Bruce what had befallen their daughters, and how they felt that they may have just met one, in the person of Sandie Wentworth.

After an hour of non-stop talking Mike finally sat back and concluded, "So as of right now, that's where we stand."

Staring at the notes that he had written whilst Mike had talked, Bruce cleared his throat and began speaking. "I am intrigued by your story Mike, and as a father I think that I might also relate to the pain of your loss, as I know how I would feel if that ever befell my children. But, as a cop you know that my next question must be, do you have any physical proof to substantiate your story?"

Knowing that this would be asked, Mike plucked his cell phone from his shirt pocket and informed Bruce that he would like to make a call.

"Calling your lawyer already," quipped a smiling Bruce.

Returning the smile, Mike informed Bruce that he was going to contact his Deputy Chief, and good friend Herman Diaz. After explaining to Herman what he would like done, Herman agreed immediately to do Mike's bidding. He advised Mike that he would call in just over an hour, and have Yolanda explain to him how to work the fax machine.

"Okay, in the meantime, I will do a little checking on the Wentworth family," glancing at his watch Bruce advised Mike and Yolanda that they certainly didn't have to wait here. He gave them directions to a highly popular Coffee and Donut place just up the street. Mike and Yolanda thanked Bruce, and happily vacated the stifling atmosphere of the small room.

SOLITARY TREE

Seated in the busy restaurant enjoying a pleasant cup of coffee, Mike and Yolanda ran through a multitude of possible scenarios that would have them meeting the girls. Glancing at his watch Mike was surprised to notice that two hours had sped by since he had talked to Herman.

Finally, Mike thought to himself as he felt his phone begin to vibrate with an in-coming call.

Seeing it was indeed Herman's number, Mike jokingly asked him if he had taken the scenic route to Mike and Yolanda's.

"Mike, this is Lieutenant William Bowers."

Shocked, Mike asked him why the fuck he's using Herman's phone.

Ignoring Mike's question, Bowers asked Mike where he's at.

"Canada," returned Mike brusquely.

"Last I heard, Canada's a pretty big place, can you be more specific please," Bowers responded sarcastically.

"A place called Vernon, in British Columbia. You still haven't answered my question Bowers. Why the fuck are you on Herman's phone?" Mike demanded harshly.

Once again ignoring Mike's question, Bowers asked Mike what Herman was doing in Mike's house.

"He was doing a favor for me," stated Mike. "What the fuck Bowers, are you in my home as well?"

"I really hate to have to tell you this Mike, your neighbors had called 9-1-1 and advised the operator that they thought they heard gunshots originating from with-in your house. When two uniforms arrived to investigate, they found the front door wide open, so they entered your home. There's no easy way to say this Mike, they found a deceased male, locating the victim's wallet they were able to identify him as Herman Diaz."

Horrified beyond measure, Mike's face clearly revealed to Yolanda that something terribly wrong had occurred.

"How soon do you think you can return," Bowers asked Mike.

SOLITARY TREE

Gauging the distance, Mike informed Bowers that since it's Monday night, they could possibly be back late Wednesday afternoon. Returning to their vehicle parked at the RCMP detachment, Mike relayed to Yolanda what had transpired.

With all thoughts regarding their daughters temporarily put on hold, Mike and Yolanda concentrated their efforts on getting back home, as quickly as possible.

They took rotating turns of four hours driving, stopping only for fuel and washroom breaks. An exhausted Yolanda finally pulled into their driveway at eight p.m. on Wednesday, the sudden cessation of the vehicles movement, caused Mike to wake from a restless nap. Advising Yolanda to remain in the vehicle, Mike crossed the short distance to the front door, ripping off the yellow police tape advising everyone that this was now a crime scene, he opened the door. Nothing could have prepared him for the destruction that had occurred in their home, it was as though ten people had been given license to wreak as much havoc as humanly possible. Gingerly walking through the devastation as it is a crime scene, Mike made his way to the safe located in the master bedroom closet, on the way he noted that the girl's pictures were conspicuously absent from their places at the kitchen table. Stepping through the doorway into the master bedroom, Mike's eyes were drawn to the large accumulation of dark red material that had soaked into the beige colored carpet. Having visited many crime scenes over his career, Mike had been insulated from the true horror of the crimes, by having no prior relationship with the victim. This did not apply here, the chalk represented where Mike's good friend, and trusted subordinate died, doing a favor for Mike. Turning his attention away from the chalk, Mike was not at all surprised to see the small safe door ajar, and clearly devoid of the important papers that had until recently resided there. Hearing a loud gasp from the area of the Livingroom, Mike quickly made his way there, quietly watching as a shocked Yolanda absorbed the wanton destruction that had occurred in their home. Crossing the few steps that separated them, Mike enfolded Yolanda into a hug, promising her they would have the house cleaned up and sold.

Pushing herself away from Mike, Yolanda shook her head. "I don't care about this Mike, all this stuff is just that, stuff. "Our good friend lost his life here doing a favor for us, if you only arrest one more murderer in your career Mike, make certain it's the asshole that killed our friend."

The funeral for Herman Diaz was a tribute to his life as a Police Officer. It was estimated that three thousand Law Enforcement Officers were present to honor Herman, there were officers present from across the nation, a large contingent of Police officers traveled south from Canada to offer their condolences, and pay homage to a fallen comrade. A distraught Yolanda and Mike paid their respects to Herman's widow Angela, expressing their sorrow that they may have been the cause of Herman's sudden and violent death.

Angela hugged the pair of them, telling them that was complete nonsense, Herman had told her on numerous occasions that his job was such that coming home at night was never guaranteed, and he was alright with that, as he strongly felt that he might be able to make a difference. Angela informed Mike and Yolanda that Herman was elated to see the two of them get together, he had always thought that they would be a good match, he also thought of Mike as the son he never had. Upon hearing this, Mike had to turn away as tears of sorrow flowed unchecked from his eyes.

Taking Mike by the arm and turning him back to face her Angela told him fiercely. "It's alright to cry today, but I want you to promise me, that beginning tomorrow you will search for Herman's killer and not stop until the day he's brought to justice."

Mike solemnly promised Angela that he would not stop until the day the killer did indeed face justice.

SOLITARY TREE

Three days after the funeral service for Herman, Mike felt his phone vibrate, retrieving it from his pants pocket he glanced at the caller ID, seeing it was an unknown number he answered it with his formal greeting. "Hello, this is Mike Chance, Chief of Detectives, Twelfth Precinct."

"Jesus Christ Mike, when did you get so fucking formal?" Even though it had been a decade since he had last heard the voice, Mike instantly knew it belonged to the man he had sworn to kill.

"What the fuck do you want Larry!" growled Mike.

"Me? Hell, buddy I don't want anything, but I may have something you want."

"What the fuck could you possibly have that I would want?" demanded Mike. "Here I thought you might be calling to tell me you have a terminal case of lead poisoning, that promised you a slow and extremely painful death."

"No Mike, sorry to disappoint, but I do happen to have in my possession certain documents, as well as the portraits of two very beautiful girls. How could someone as ugly as you, possibly create something so beautiful, perhaps the credit belongs to your ex-wife Adele."

Assimilating the information offered by Larry, Mike realized that Larry was the killer. "You miserable fuck! You were at the house," hissed Mike.

"Well yes, I had heard from credible sources that you and your flunky were out of town, so I thought that I would have a little look- see into your life. Imagine my surprise when I heard the front door open, and in walked a whistling Herman. He was so intent on whatever the fuck he was doing, he didn't even notice the mud from my shoes on the floor.

SOLITARY TREE

Well I just sort of hung back, and watched while he dug around in your tennis shoes looking for the safe combination. By the way Mike, he didn't appreciate having to dig around in your smelly shoes. Once he had the safe open, I simply stepped forward and thanked him for his trouble.

What nothing to say Mike?", as though defending his indefensible actions Larry continued. "I gave him a choice Mike, I told him that he could leave and it would be our little secret. The stupid fuck refused my offer, told me that he would know that he had backed down, and he couldn't live with that.

He told me there's only one way that it could end, telling me that since he had left his weapon at home, the least I could do was shoot straight. He died well, I will give him that much."

With his hatred for Larry boiling to the surface, Mike was temporarily speechless.

"Tell you what Mike. If you would like to have this property of yours returned, why don't we meet somewhere quiet for a reunion."

Knowing that Larry would already have a location picked out, Mike growled a single word. "Where?"

When Larry described the meeting place Mike knew it well, knew that it's remote location would guarantee that there would be no interference. "So how about we meet there about six o'clock tomorrow morning."

Not bothering to answer him, Mike ended the call.

Tapping his phone thoughtfully against his thigh, Mike made a call. "I'm coming by I will be there in twenty minutes. Mike then described to the listener what he needed."

"It will be ready," responded the listener.

Having had no contact with Larry Donovan for the last decade, Mike thought that he could still safely predict his ex-partner's moves. Calling Yolanda, he was relieved to hear the call go to her voice mail, since he was sure the ever-perceptive Yolanda would hear in his voice what he was about to-do.

SOLITARY TREE

Grabbing a quick bite to eat at a fast food joint, Mike headed to the pre-arranged meeting place. He knew that he was in for a very long night, but he also knew that Larry would get there at least two hours before the arranged time. Locating the empty building, Mike was not surprised to see the building was even more decrepit then he remembered.

After scrutinizing the front door and the undisturbed layer of dust that covered everything, Mike retired to the back of the building in search of an entry point. Once inside the building, Mike rehearsed the moves he thought Larry would make, nodding his head at the scenario he thought Larry might follow, Mike found a vantage point to begin his wait.

The noise of someone stealthily opening the front door of the building woke Mike from his light nap. Glancing at his watch Mike could see that it was just slightly before four a.m., bingo he thought right on time. Mike then closed his eyes, if he's right Larry's next move would be to turn on the lights to study the layout, and find a vantage point. Mike couldn't help but grin as he heard Larry suddenly curse with pain as his leg struck something, sure enough even though his eyes were closed Mike could sense the building was now flooded with light. Slowly opening his eyes to allow them to adjust, Mike grinned like a Wolf when from his uncomfortable perch on the second-floor cat-walk, he watched as Larry found the best place to hide. Deciding that he had observed his ex-partner long enough, Mike lightly tapped the barrel of the muzzle suppressor against the iron railing. It was almost comical watching Larry freeze, as he digested the sound he had heard, and attempted to interpret its meaning.

"Mike?", he asked still facing the opposite wall from whence the sound had originated.

"None other," replied Mike calmly.

"When did you get here?" Larry asked.

"Before you did," answered Mike simply.

SOLITARY TREE

"Alright if I turn around?"

"Of course, how rude of me not to extend you that courtesy, please accept my apologies, and just so you don't do something stupid keep your arms away from your body," ordered Mike in a lethal voice.

"Jesus Mike, have you ever gotten gray, whatever happened to the jet-black hair?"

"We're not here to discuss my hair Larry," responded Mike coldly.

Nodding his direction in the vague direction of the weapon in Mike's hand, Larry commented on the fact that it didn't resemble the standard Police issued firearm.

"You're right Larry it's not. I have some friends that were more than accommodating, fortunately for me they are not bound by the same laws that I adhere to. It seems that these people have a long memory, and they didn't appreciate the fact that you attempted to blackmail them some years back. Speaking of old friends, I was informed that Curly showed up on the Medical Examiners table, his chest looked like someone decided to use him as a carving board, I guess you wouldn't know anything about that would you Larry."

"The stupid fuck should have stayed in the Witness Protection Program, I had just about given up on ever seeing him again, when lo and behold there he was. He should have known when he gave me up to the cops that I would be looking for him, if he had just kept his mouth shut he would be still alive."

"Did you bring those documents?" asked Mike.

"Mike, it would have been incredibly stupid on my part if I had brought those documents with me, I may be many things, but stupid is not one of them."

"I would argue that point with you Larry, I truly believe you are an incredibly stupid human being. You showed up here this morning and were actually foolish enough to believe that I would allow you to leave here alive."

SOLITARY TREE

Laughing uneasily at this solemn declaration, Larry reminded Mike that if he died, Mike would never recover the documents.

"See Larry, that's the reason I believe you are truly stupid, the only proof I need, is at this minute flowing nicely through my veins. Those documents, they were the icing on the cake, granted they may have helped but they are not necessary.
Larry, you fail to comprehend that you are not leaving here alive, the minute you called and set up this meeting your fate was sealed," avowed Mike in the same cold voice.

"That's funny Mike, you're a fuckin sheep, and sheep don't do that," voiced Larry becoming uncomfortably aware that this was a different Mike then the one that used to be his former partner.

Tapping the suppressor lightly against the railing, Mike solemnly informed Larry that someone else had suffered from that very same misconception, and that person was no longer living.

"Are you going to be as brave as my friend and ask me to shoot straight," asked Mike as casually as if he was asking the time of day.

"That's funny Mike, you're the paragon of right and wrong, and even if you thought you were right, you wouldn't have the fucking balls to shoot me in cold blood," snorted Larry derisively.

"Your dead wrong Larry," with that said, Mike pulled the trigger twice in quick succession. The resultant noise was no louder than someone suffering from a minor case of hiccups. Rising from his seated position, Mike casually walked down the stairs to the inert form of Larry, where he fired three more bullets into the already dead body. Staring at Larry's corpse with fathomless, ice cold black eyes that revealed no emotion whatsoever, Mike spoke softly. "She's not my flunky asshole, she's my salvation."

SOLITARY TREE

Walking outside, Mike peeled the tight fitting black leather gloves off, he discarded them together with the weapon into the fast moving, highly polluted river that flowed behind the building.

Knowing that it was only just after five a.m. he placed the call anyways. "Good morning Angela, this is Mike Chance calling, I apologize for the early hour, I promised you I would not rest until I brought Herman's killer to justice, it gives me great pleasure to inform you that justice has been served."

CHAPTER TWENTY-TWO

"Jesus Christ!" uttered Barry Wentworth in denial. "Are you sure that's necessary? Jas is young and strong, I'm sure she will be able to get well on her own."

The look of concern on the cherubic face of Dr. Rob Blenkinsop, who specialized in compromised Renal systems, was mute testimony to the gravity of Jasmine's prognosis.

"Despite our best efforts with drug therapy, and carefully monitoring her diet, Jasmine's Kidneys are still failing badly. In Jasmine's best interests she will begin Kidney Dialysis immediately, and will in my opinion require it four times a week. I truly believe that we need to act with some urgency, at this unprecedented rate of failure, I predict that Jasmine will require a Kidney transplant sooner rather than later."

While Barry and Jackie absorbed this shocking news, Rob opened a drawer in his desk and removed some papers. Gently clearing his throat to get their attention, he began to explain the next step they needed to take, placing the papers he had secured from his desk drawer in front of Barry and Jackie, he explained what they represented. "I know your daughters were adopted, therefore there is an unfortunate gap in their medical history. In a perfect world, Jasmine's sister Sandie, would have been the ideal candidate to donate an organ, but her age negates that option. I will have Jasmine's name placed on the waiting list for a Kidney Transplant but, there are no guarantees an acceptable donor will be located."

SOLITARY TREE

Pointing to the papers Jackie asked the sympathetic doctor where they needed to sign, and were there any actions that herself and Barry could undertake to expedite locating an acceptable donor.

"I'm sorry to say, that unfortunately there is nothing that you can do now," allowing himself a small pensive smile he added. "Unless of course you are able to contact a living relative of the girls. As I stated even though her name will be on the waiting list, it's a very long list. The medical community has been attempting to impress upon the Government, that urgent steps are needed to raise the public's awareness of this impending crisis. I would like to ask you not as the parents of a child suffering from Kidney failure, but rather as ordinary adults, were you aware of this issue before Jasmine encountered her illness?"

Jackie quickly spoke up, informing Rob that even though she was a registered nurse she had been completely ignorant of this issue.

"I certainly don't expect the two of you to jump onto a soap box and begin haranguing people about this dilemma, but during the course of your daily lives perhaps mentioning to your friends and family members to register as donors, would in some small way help."

Shaking Rob's hand, and thanking him for the care he's extending to their daughter, Jackie and Barry took their leave.

Taking the stairs to the third floor of the Hospital where Jasmine would be receiving her dialysis treatment, Barry and Jackie watched as the nurses quickly and efficiently prepared the wan looking Jasmine for her treatment.

When Jasmine's treatment was underway, Barry kissed Jackie lightly on the cheek, and advised her that he needed to go to the office for a while.

SOLITARY TREE

Nodding a mute greeting to his secretary, Barry ensconced himself in his office, when faced with a problem with-in his business network Barry would unconsciously begin tapping his pen lightly against his lower lip. His business associates were aware of this habit, and they knew that when the tapping started the solution to a problem was not far off. Re-playing in his mind the recent conversation with Jasmine's specialist, Barry's thoughts became fixated when recalling the fact that his daughter was at the bottom of a very long waiting list. He knew that he would have no compunctions whatsoever regarding the means used to secure a matching Kidney for Jas. Life, like business, is driven by money, either the lack of it, or acquiring more of it, realizing this simple fact, and being willing to exploit it, in most cases meant the difference between success and failure. It was not reasonable to expect someone to watch their child waste away, just because of a long list. With this thought, Barry knew beyond a doubt that out there somewhere, would be someone with a kidney that would be a perfect match for Jas, and who for the right incentives would be willing to part with it. Jotting down a note to call his lawyer, Barry noticed the red light on his phone blinking, indicating his secretary was attempting to contact him.

"Yes, Bernice, what is it?" asked Barry impatiently.

"Barry, the Mayor is on line one."

Surprised by her response, Barry thanked her and wondering what the Mayor of their fine community was calling about picked up his phone. "Mr. Mayor, this is indeed a surprise, how may I be of service?"

"Hello Barry," chortling lightly at being called Mr. Mayor by someone he had known all his life, he insisted that Barry call him by his given name of Allan. He explained to Barry that he would greatly appreciate it if Barry could tear himself away from his desk long enough, to attend a meeting in the mayor's office at three p.m. that afternoon.

"Certainly Allan, I will be there," replied a mildly curious Barry.

SOLITARY TREE

As requested, Barry arrived at the mayor's receptionist at exactly three p.m. He was surprised when he was immediately ushered into the mayor's office, entering the rather lavish office for the first time, Barry quickly absorbed the numerous photographic prints of local orchards that adorned the walls. It was then he noticed they were not alone, rising from two couches placed alongside a large window that overlooked the water fountain in the town square, were acquaintances of Barry that represented a cross section of business leaders in Vernon.

After shaking the Mayor's hand and thanking him for the invitation, Barry politely greeted the other people in attendance.

Once the greetings were completed the Mayor invited everyone to re-take their seats, indicating to Barry that there was a separate chair for him. Still confused by this meeting that included of all people, the superintendent of the local RCMP detachment, Barry was not left in the dark for very long.

"As you all know," began the mayor. "I will not be seeking another term in this November's civic election. I believe it's time for some new blood that perhaps might steer the community in a new direction. I have been honored to serve these last three terms, but my wife has informed me that she wishes to travel abroad, so to that end I have been making some discreet enquiries. It gives me great pleasure Barry, to state unequivocally that your name was mentioned far too many times to ignore. Those of us gathered here today would be very pleased if you were to allow your name to stand for Mayor this November."

The applause that followed this announcement was both unanimous and sincere.

Barry was caught completely off guard by this announcement, he like everyone in the tightly knit community had heard rumors to the affect that Allan would not be seeking re-election. He had assumed this meeting might be an opportunity for the Mayor to toss some names at Barry, he certainly did not expect his name to be the one tossed.

SOLITARY TREE

With the mayor gently nudging him, Barry rose from his chair and warmly thanked everyone present for this honor. "You have caught me completely off-guard." admitted a very humble Barry. "This was the last thing I ever expected, if this had occurred even three months ago, I would have gladly allowed my name to stand on the ballot for Mayor. Unfortunately, my eldest daughter Jasmine is involved in what could be the fight of her life, she has suffered a catastrophic Kidney disease which will require a Kidney transplant as soon as possible. I'm sure most of you know that Jackie and myself adopted our two precious daughters, so we lack any information regarding other family members that could possibly be donors. As of right now Jasmine's name sits at the very bottom, of a very long list of people in need of a kidney transplant. So regrettably, I feel that with all my energies devoted to our daughter's well-being, I would have to decline this gracious offer."

Barry's audience was captivated by this news, there had been no inkling that Jasmine was this ill. As one they rose to their feet and offered hope and support for Jasmine, Barry was touched by this out- pouring of compassion for his daughter.

With the Mayor requesting that he stay behind, Barry stood at the large glass window gazing at the water fountain, while the Mayor said his goodbyes to his departing friends.

"I sincerely apologize Barry, that was extremely tactless on my behalf, I just wish I had known Jasmine was that ill."

"No need to apologize Allan, you couldn't possibly have known."

"Well, I know my wife would share this sentiment, when I say that I hope she has a full and speedy recovery."

"There is one thing Allan that everyone can do to help, and that is fill out an organ donor card, it only takes a few minutes to do yet it could save someone's life."

SOLITARY TREE

 With a perplexed expression on his face Allan replied. "Jesus Barry, I had never given it a thought."

 "That's alright Allan, neither had we," murmured Barry as he left the Mayor's office.

CHAPTER TWENTY-THREE

Knocking on the closed door of Detachment Superintendent Gregory Lamont's door, Staff Sergeant Bruce Hanley waited until he heard the polished voice of his boss invite him to enter. Although there was a significant difference in rank between these two men, their mutual respect transcended the difference in rank. At times like these, when the two of them enjoyed a private moment, Greg insisted that Bruce drop the Sir and call him by his name.

"What do you think of that Barry fellow as a possible new mayor?" queried Bruce.

"He may not run, apparently, his daughter is very ill and he felt that he could not serve the community properly," responded Greg to his Sergeant's question.

"Well I think I can tell right off that he would not be right for the job, he's way too honest," joked Bruce.

"Yes, you have a point there alright Bruce, I have known the family for some years, and the Wentworth's pride themselves on the fact that their word is worth more than any written contract."

With that said they quickly moved on to the more pressing needs of the detachment.

Almost exactly a week had passed since Bruce and Greg had discussed Barry Wentworth, and not being available to run on the mayor's ballot due to a sick child, when something jogged Bruce's memory.

SOLITARY TREE

Locating his notebook, he thumbed through it until he found what he was looking for, reading the notes that he had jotted down, he stared at the notebook as though the answer he sought might leap off the page, it was then he decided to do a little digging. After conducting several casual sounding phone interviews, and one where he was slightly less than truthful to obtain information regarding the sick Wentworth child, Bruce began to feel that he was onto something very big. Walking down the short hallway in the detachment building to Greg's office, Bruce was dismayed to learn that his boss would be tied up for several hours. With nothing too pressing to do, Bruce waited impatiently for his boss to become available, finally after what seemed an eternity he was granted a meeting with Greg.

 Greg proved to be just as intrigued as Bruce was when he heard what had befallen Mikael Chance and his daughters. When Bruce arrived at the point in the narrative where Mike, and Yolanda thought they had met his youngest missing daughter, co-incidentally her name turned out to be Sandie Wentworth. At this point, Greg sat up straighter and began taking notes of his own. "What happened to this Mike and Yolanda?" questioned Greg.

 Scratching his head in puzzlement, Bruce informed Greg that when the interview had concluded, Mike was contacting a friend back home to fax the identification of the girls to this office. "I never heard from them again, I checked the resort they were vacationing at, and was told they had left in a hurry," reported a baffled Bruce. "Now I know that I might be completely wrong with my hypothesis but, this Mike Chance whose identification stated he was Chief of Detectives for the Twelfth Precinct in Metro-City is a big Asian guy.

SOLITARY TREE

Co-incidentally both Wentworth daughters are Asian, he was positive that Sandie Wentworth was his daughter, he had an artist do age enhanced portraits and from what Mike and Yolanda claimed, Sandie Wentworth resembled almost exactly what the artist had portrayed.

"There are numerous what-ifs in your hypothesis Bruce," stated an unconvinced Greg. "We have nothing other than this guy's gut instinct that Sandie Wentworth is his daughter. He was supposed to have scientific evidence faxed here, but instead disappeared. I have worked with you for too many years, to think that you are basing your conclusions solely on the word of this American cop," smiling indulgently at his Staff Sergeant, Greg asked for the information Bruce had thus far failed to provide.

"I made a couple of calls, it seems that the elder Wentworth daughter is suffering from a rare kidney disease, her kidneys have all but ceased to function. If it's true that this American cop is in fact her father, there's a better than even chance that he could be a kidney donor, and potentially save her life. What I would like to propose, is before we inform the Wentworth's of this development, we have Chance either return here for a blood test, or have blood work completed there, with the results being sent here."

As Greg carefully weighed what Bruce had so eloquently stated, he decided that there would be no harm in proceeding in the way that Bruce had proposed. "Do it!" he ordered brusquely. "Contact Chance and inform him that for us to continue to further investigate this case, he needs to submit a blood sample to prove paternity, failure to do so will negate any assistance we might provide in this case. Do not, under any circumstances inform him of the girl's condition, the last thing we need is some hysterical American cop running amok."

Having Greg's permission to proceed, Bruce immediately set the wheels in motion, and hit a brick wall.

SOLITARY TREE

He was in possession of Chance's cell phone number which he called repeatedly for two days, the only response this elicited was the click of the call being ended, he couldn't even reach the man's voice mail.

He had no more luck when he contacted the Precinct itself, after identifying who he was, he clearly heard the person at the other end of the call, issue a loud hoot of derision as they hung up on him. It was only through his stubborn determination not to give up that he was finally rewarded, on what he swore would be his last attempt to contact Chance, the man himself answered.

"This is Chance."

"Is this Mike Chance, Chief of Detectives for the Twelfth Precinct?"

"Yes, it is."

"This is Bruce Hanley, Staff Sergeant of the RCMP detachment located in Vernon, British Columbia. We spoke some time ago about your missing daughters, you informed this office that you suspected Sandie Wentworth might be one of your missing children. I'm not sure what has happened in the interim, but the last time we spoke I was under the impression that you were going to make available to this office, evidence that would prove Sandie Wentworth was your child."

"Yes, I was, but that evidence has been lost to me, there have been developments down here, the DNA and fingerprint profiles I had, are no longer in my possession."

As Bruce weighed this revelation, the cynicism that existed in all cops rose to the surface. "That seems somewhat convenient, Mr. Chance. You present yourself here at the Detachment, you insist that one of our local girls is your daughter who disappeared ten years ago, and that you have in your possession evidence to back your claim. Then like a puff of smoke, you disappear and now you claim your evidence has also disappeared. If you were me, what would you be thinking right about now."

SOLITARY TREE

"Yes, I fully appreciate what you're saying Bruce," responded Mike grudgingly, knowing full well that if roles were reversed he would label Bruce as delusional.

"As of right now it's not possible for me to return to Vernon, what I would like to suggest Bruce, is I go to a lab, have bloodwork done and send the results to you. I'm positive that the results when compared to Desiree's, I'm sorry, I guess her name is now Sandie, anyways I'm sure they will prove beyond a doubt I'm her biological father."

"Mike, you seem to be missing my main point. You have not proven to me that your girls were abducted, right now, all I have is the fact that you showed up here and claimed that Sandie Wentworth is your child. For all I know you could have voluntarily placed them with an adoption agency, and now for reasons known only to yourself, you wish to have them returned. Before I proceed any further with this file I will need verification that your children were indeed taken illegally, perhaps you have undertaken a search for the girls, and having located them, know that your paternity suit would be proven."

Knowing that Bruce was asking all the right questions, did nothing to ease the searing anger he was beginning to feel towards this Canadian cop. "For fuck sakes Bruce are you sitting near a computer terminal?" questioned Mike, venting his anger at the Canadian cop.

"Yes, I'm at my desk."

"Using your search engine, go to Jacobs convicted of Human Trafficking. You will see pictures of my two daughters and of myself."

Mike could hear the audible click of the keyboard through the phone as Bruce hammered away at the keys.

Following a few minutes of dead air as he perused the report on the conviction of the Jacob's couple, Bruce acknowledged the fact that he was now convinced Mike had been truthful.

SOLITARY TREE

Knowing the severity of Jasmine Wentworth's condition, and with Greg's warning about not having a crazed American cop wreaking havoc, Bruce attempted to be exceedingly circumspect when he advised Mike that the blood work should be done sooner rather than later."

With his earlier anger dissipated, Mike started what was easily the hardest conversation of his life. "I'm not sure that I have the right to interfere in their lives Bruce. It has been a decade now since they were taken, I can only hope that they are still together. Watching Desiree at the resort it was easy to tell that she was a well-adjusted teenager, she appeared to be quite happy. My life has been a constant source of loss, my parents were killed, a kind and decent friend of mine was killed in a planned hit and run. My ex-wife blamed me when our daughters were taken, maybe she was right, since the people that were involved in the abduction hated me."

This revealing, deeply introspective glimpse into Mike's character, portrayed someone who was genuinely at war with their emotions.

Endeavoring to maintain the façade of an impartial third party, Bruce explained to Mike it would only take a few minutes to have the bloodwork completed, have it sent North, and we will establish whether Sandie is indeed your child or not. At that point in time Mike could make his decision.

Agreeing to this strategy, Mike advised Bruce that he would have it completed right away.

CHAPTER TWENTY-FOUR

Signing for, and accepting the sealed courier's envelope, Bruce entered his office and opened it, inside was what Bruce assumed to be Mike Chance's bloodwork results. Being thoroughly unfamiliar with medical data, Bruce photocopied the three documents enclosed with-in the envelope, placing the originals in his filing cabinet for safe keeping. With a large black felt pen, Bruce began to redact any information that was not directly related to Mike chance's blood type, pleased with the result, Bruce informed his secretary that he will be out of the office for a while.

At first Bruce headed in the direction of his car, but deciding that with the day being so nice he would walk the short distance to his friend Rob Blenkinsop's office.

"Hey Bruce! What brings you here in the middle of the day? I also see that you're dressed up in your finest," joked the cherubic Doctor as he warmly shook his friends hand in greeting.

"Hello yourself Rob, still sore from Sunday's round of golf?" teased the genial Bruce.

Inviting him into his private office, Rob shot an inquisitive glance at the envelope that Bruce carried. What do you have their buddy? I was sure I had paid my speeding tickets, remember if you arrest me you won't have a partner for Sundays golf match," teased Rob good naturedly.

SOLITARY TREE

Seating himself at the small round coffee table at the far end of Rob's office Bruce stretched out his long legs and began to laugh. "I wish I had of thought of that myself Buddy, but no that's not what I have here." Having concluded their usual ritual of tongue in cheek humor, Bruce turned serious. "I have been told that you are young Jasmine Wentworth's doctor, I have also been told that she is amid a serious medical situation." Tapping the envelope lightly against the edge of the table Bruce continued to speak slowly and succinctly to his friend. "I would greatly appreciate it if you would look at the blood type that I have here, and compare it to Jasmine's with respect to a match. Rest assured Rob, I would never ask you to anything that could be remotely construed as unethical or illegal," with that said he passed the envelope to his friend.

Rising from the chair opposite his friend, Rob moved to his filing cabinet, returning shortly with a thick file. Extracting the report from the envelope, he was surprised at the excessive amount of black ink, raising an eyebrow quizzically at Bruce he asked. "Did you use up the year's budget on markers?" Knowing full well that his friend was being sarcastic, Bruce did not dignify the question with an answer.

Closing his eyes during the time that Rob required to carefully analyze the report, Bruce envisioned the many different ramifications the report could generate. Some of them good, some of them not so good.

"This report is extremely interesting Bruce," lifting his gaze to stare at his friend as though he were a magician, Rob continued in a voice that betrayed his level of excitement. "Please feel free to correct me if I'm wrong, the Wentworth girls were adopted, the parents have no inkling as to their background, yet you waltz in here with a report that leaves no doubt whatsoever in my mind that whoever supplied this sample is either a sibling or a parent," tapping the report with a chubby forefinger, Rob declared that whoever supplied this blood sample would be the best possible match that Jasmine could ever hope for.

SOLITARY TREE

Scrutinizing his friend for any clue as to what Bruce was thinking, Rob soon realized that his friends stony countenance would give up nothing.

Rising from the comfortable chair, Bruce held out his hand for the report, accepting the page from Rob, he advised his friend that there will be many ramifications resulting from this report. Shaking his friends hand, Bruce thanked him for his time adding. "For now, pretend you have never seen the report. There are steps that need to be taken before this report can see the light of day, rest assured that Jasmine's best interests are first and foremost in whatever happens.

Smiling broadly at Bruce, Rob asked him. "What report, I haven't laid eyes on my golfing buddy since Sunday."

Enjoying the warm sun on his face, Bruce strolled back to the detachment at a leisurely pace, back in his office he was inundated with personnel issues that demanded his immediate attention, thus preventing him moving forward with the Chance file until seventeen hundred. Delving once more into this intriguing file, Bruce was astounded that after ten long years, Chance discovered his girls wholly by accident while on vacation. With the file, open on his desk, Bruce commenced writing down the sequential order in which he thought this file should proceed. Perusing his notes, he was pleased as he visualized a positive ending to this file.

"Chance!"

"Hello Mike, this is Bruce Hanley calling from Vernon, British Columbia."

"Yes, your accent gives you away every time," chuckled Mike.

Refusing to rise to the bait concerning accents, Bruce informed Mike that the bloodwork was indeed a match. He did not see the need right now, to inform Mike they had compared the results to Jasmine's, not Sandie's. Bearing in mind Greg's warning about having a crazed American cop wreaking havoc, Bruce was extremely circumspect when he advised Mike that the sooner Yolanda and Mike could return to Vernon the better.

SOLITARY TREE

"Hang on a second Bruce, I'm still at the office, as is Yolanda. I'm sure she can have an answer for you right away," barely a minute had passed when Mike informed Bruce they would fly into a place called Kelowna, at thirteen hundred tomorrow. "Would you like to be met by one of our officers?"

"No thank-you, we will rent a car, Yolanda thinks it's just a short drive north to Vernon."

"That's correct, it's only just over thirty-minutes, barring any unforeseen developments you should arrive here at the detachment, no later than fourteen hundred tomorrow."

"Sounds good Bruce, we will see you tomorrow, and by the way thank-you," Mike remarked unable to mask the excitement in his voice.

CHAPTER TWENTY-FIVE

Upon their arrival, at the Vernon RCMP detachment at almost exactly fourteen hundred, Yolanda and Mike were warmly greeted by Bruce. Politely enquiring how their flight was, Bruce escorted them to the detachment's second floor boardroom. Advising the pair that he needed to return downstairs to await the arrival of another party, Bruce invited Yolanda and Mike to help themselves to the assorted refreshments available in the refrigerator, and coffee was ready in the silver urn on the counter.

Leaving the two guests to fend for themselves, Bruce returned downstairs to await the arrival of the tardy Rob Blenkinsop, he was beginning to feel what the conductor of an orchestra must feel, as the many individual instruments are forged into one, and the ensuing magic created by the ensemble.

Spotting his rather portly cherubic friend entering the detachment's main foyer, Bruce hurried over to him and with a perfunctory greeting whisked him upstairs.

Once again entering the boardroom, Bruce noticed that Yolanda had a sparkling water in front of her, and Mike was sipping from a bottle of lemonade. "Okay folks," began Bruce knowing that he was well past the point of no return. "I would like to introduce you to Dr. Rob Blenkinsop," Bruce was not in the least bit surprised when Mike and Yolanda's eyebrows raised in puzzlement when he mentioned Doctor. "I will now allow Rob with his expertise to chair the meeting."

Rob began by informing Mike and Yolanda that he had been the one to ascertain if Mike's DNA markers in his bloodwork matched the girls.

Seizing on this minor slip-up, Mike immediately looked at Bruce. "Girls?" he demanded. "Are both our daughters here?"

With the realization that his friend and inadvertently slipped up, Bruce once again assumed control of the meeting. Taking his time, he explained that the reason Rob was invited to attend this meeting is because he is Jasmine's Doctor. Having explained to Mike and Yolanda, Jasmine's prognosis and the complications that have arisen from the Kidney disease, Rob concluded his ten-minute monologue stating. "The disease has ravaged her Kidneys, the need for a transplant is paramount to her survival."

With an intuitive glance at Rob, Mike asked softly. "What is it you're not telling us?"

At this point in time Bruce stepped in again, and speaking just as softly, advised Mike and Yolanda that Jasmine is Sandie's older sister.

Though Mike had suspected as much when Rob was informing them of her condition, he was still overwhelmed to learn that both their daughters were still together. Feeling Yolanda's hand squeeze his forearm, and hearing a small groan, Mike's determination to reserve his tears for a private moment, melted the instant he witnessed large tears spill from her eyes, and cascade down her cheeks.

Nudging Rob, Bruce motioned towards the door, informing Yolanda and Mike they would be just outside.

The scene that unfolded inside the boardroom, visibly displayed the undying love that parents feel for children. Yolanda and Mike were ecstatic, they clung to each other with the knowledge that soon they would be reunited with the girls.

SOLITARY TREE

Hearing a subtle knock on the door, Mike rose from his chair and opening the door, invited the two waiting men back into the room. Once everyone was seated Mike asked Rob if he was a suitable match for Jasmine's kidney transplant.

"You sir, represent every doctor's dream of a donor. You are as close to a perfect match that Jasmine could hope for.

My question to you is, are you willing to donate one of your kidneys to her?"

"How soon can you set it up?" returned a deadly serious Mike. "If you can do it tonight, I'm more than ready!"

Beaming at Mike's eagerness, Rob promised him that as soon as he knows, he will let Mike know.

At this juncture, Bruce thanked Rob for his time and escorted him from the room, with Rob promising Mike, that he will be in touch, as there is a small mountain of paperwork that needs to be completed before a date can be set for the transplant.

Expecting Bruce to return alone, Mike, and Yolanda were startled when he returned with another couple in tow. After introducing the Wentworth's to the Chances, Bruce explained that they were the adoptive parents of Jasmine and Sandie.

Glaring at the couple, with undisguised loathing, Mike jumped up from his chair with the intention of hurdling the table that stood between them, and attack Barry. "How is it that you fucking adopted my children, and not know that there was something amiss in the proceedings. Or did you do what the Jacobs did, and just fuckin buy them," roared Mike, allowing a decade of frustration to fuel his rage.

Bruce abruptly admonished Mike, stating that he will have several RCMP members attend the meeting, if Mike was unable to curb his violence.

"Just who in the fuck do you think you are?" demanded an equally incensed Barry unafraid of Mike's wrath. "You show up here out of the fuckin blue, and begin making inflammatory accusations against my wife and myself," not intimidated in the least by Mike's barely restrained violence, the usually unflappable Barry continued speaking in a tone of voice that was completely alien to his wife.

"We fucking rescued your children from a guy that considered them merchandise, if it weren't for us who knows what might have befallen those two beautiful girls. We were cognizant of the fact that there were holes in his story, but we were also not aware that these children had been abducted, we had to accept his story at face value," almost spitting saliva in his rage Barry continued his unremitting attack on Mike. "Two minutes after we first saw the girls they took ownership of our hearts, Jackie and I knew that in paying that sonofabitch for the girls we might be committing some type of crime, but the alternative of allowing that guy to maintain custody of the girls, was by far the worst of the two," temporarily halting his attack on Mike, Barry took several deep breaths endeavoring to gain control of his emotions. In a slightly more restrained voice Barry concluded his tirade by informing Yolanda and Mike, that, if they thought they were going to wrest the girls from himself and Jackie, they had better be prepared for the fight of their lives. "We have forged a strong united family, the girls represent everything that we love, we have shared many moments that will be treasured for the rest of our lives. Jasmine is currently facing what could be a life-threatening disease, you two could not have possibly picked a worse time to show up." Sensing that her husband had concluded his tirade, Jackie informed Mike and Yolanda, that they had been prepared to sell everything they owned, to secure the girls freedom from the repulsive man whose care they were in.

Though inwardly seething at Mike and Yolanda, Jackie refused to allow them to see how distraught she was with the idea that she may lose her daughters; therefore, displaying an outwardly calm, quiet demeanor, Jackie told them that it was she that had demanded of Barry to do whatever it took to secure the girls freedom.

At this point, Bruce once again leaped into the fray, advising the Wentworth's that Mike's blood type had proven to be a perfect match to Jasmine, declaring that Mike has already agreed to be the donor.

Mike broke the ensuing pregnant silence following Bruce's declaration, speaking directly to Barry Wentworth. "I came here today fully prepared to cause you severe bodily harm; I have ten years of hatred seeking release. Irrespective of our host Bruce, I was intent on exacting revenge for the time lost with my daughters. However, having only just met you, I realize that instead of selfishly seeking revenge I should be thanking you for providing a safe and loving home for our daughters. The means in which the girls came to live with you, I belatedly realize are irrelevant, what I must not lose sight of is, you accepted complete stranger's children into your home and showered them with love, kindness, and provided them with a secure environment in which to grow-up." Mike swiftly strode the length of the table and approaching Jackie, requested her permission to demonstrate his eternal debt by bestowing a hug upon her.

More than a little intimidated by the sheer size of Mike, Jackie stood up and accepted what Mike had offered. Turning his attention to Barry, Mike extended his hand whilst thanking him for being the father that Mike had failed to be. Returning to his seat Mike kissed Yolanda warmly on the cheek.

Watching the formidable size of Mike return to his chair on the opposite side of the table, Barry knew that if he would have suffered grievous injury, if Mike had acted on his impulse to attack Barry. Directing his gaze towards Bruce seated at the head of the table, Barry questioned Bruce's statement about Mike being a perfect transplant match for Jas.

Bruce than relayed to Barry that when Mike and Yolanda had approached the RCMP to aid in their search, Mike provided a blood sample that proved to be an exact match to Jasmine.

SOLITARY TREE

"And the reason we weren't privy to this?" questioned Barry.
 "Well to be honest Barry, I originally thought it was hoax, Mike and Yolanda had presented themselves here with some wild tale about meeting their long-lost daughter, they then disappeared into thin air. I had serious misgivings about mentioning this until there was concrete proof provided. This proof was established just yesterday, and though some might question the legality of the actions I took, I feel vindicated by the fact that we are all sitting in the same room, with the perfect donor for Jasmine also present," concluded Bruce. Sensing the anger that had earlier threatened to extinguish any hopes Bruce had harbored about the two couples becoming affable had been dispensed with, Bruce excused himself from the room, thus allowing the four-people privacy to discuss the girls.
 With the two couples now able to comprehend that love for the girls was the paramount emotion in the room, they relaxed their guards, and begin to learn about the journeys they had shared with the girls.
 Mike apprised Jackie and Barry that he had many times considered suicide, but acknowledged that by doing so meant that he had relinquished any hope of locating his girls. Jackie and Barry chuckled when Mike related to them the whimsical urge that propelled him to visit a fortune teller, they were amazed when he admitted that both him and Yolanda had seen almost exactly what the fortune teller had predicted nearly a decade ago.
 When Jackie re-lived the moment Barry and herself first laid eyes on the girls, and the condition that they were in, Mike and Yolanda felt tears well from their eyes.
 The four then discussed in great depth the up-coming transplant for Jasmine, being a registered nurse Jackie informed Mike and Yolanda that best case scenario, the operation will take place in a month. Jackie stated unequivocally that their trust in Rob was absolute. "He is an incredible Doctor who came highly recommended."

SOLITARY TREE

When Jackie had mentioned that it could take up to one month to perform the transplant, Mike and Yolanda were clearly distressed, wondering if the delay would pose an additional risk to Jasmine's already deteriorating health.

Understanding and appreciating their concern, Jackie related to them this wait time was standard, and that Jasmine's health will not significantly decrease due to the wait.

The four then discussed at what point in time, it would be best for Mike and Yolanda to officially meet the girls, the unanimous consensus was, that Jasmine's interests would be best served by waiting until after the surgery.

The mood in the room could be cautiously described as congenial, on the one hand you no longer have two people who feared the loss of their beloved daughters, and on the other hand the Father who realized that the people sitting across from him loved his daughters as much, if not more than he did.

The meeting adjourned with both couples agreeing to meet tomorrow at lunch, as Jackie was sure that by then Rob would have a date in place for the operation.

The next day when the two couples met for lunch at Barry and Jackie's favorite eating place, Jackie confirmed to Mike and Yolanda the date set by Rob for the transplant. It was as Jackie had thought almost a month away, with that in mind Mike and Yolanda thought they would return home, to prepare for a lengthy stay upon their return to Vernon.

CHAPTER TWENTY-SIX

Feeling an irritating, incessant poking to his shoulder, Mike reluctantly left the warm comfortable place he was in, and began to claw his way back upwards through the many layers of subterranean consciousness. At last, after what seemed an interminable journey, Mike was welcomed back to full consciousness when he felt a burning sensation on his lower right side, reaching down with his hand to rub the burn away, he was surprised to feel the rough texture of a large wound dressing, where there should have been smooth skin. It was at that moment his memory having also partially shaken off a small portion of the anesthesia, reminded him that he had just donated a kidney. Having yet to discover the source of the irritating poke, Mike finally opened one eye, and in the shadowy darkness of the dimly lit room spied a pair eyes equally as black as Mike's staring at him. The lingering hangover effects of the anesthesia did not allow Mike to be startled, what they did allow was a tiny stupid looking grin to appear on his face when he asked the young lady if she was an angel.

Staring at Mike through her jet-black eyes, with an expression on her face as if she were studying an alien insect, Sandie finally asked. "Are you my father?"

With a throat and mouth utterly parched to the point that speech was impossible, Mike pointed in the direction of a small cup with a drinking straw protruding from it, miming a drinking motion.

Passing the cup to him, Sandie continued to stare unabashedly at Mike absorbing their obvious similarities, skin the color of toffee, eyes that are as black as a moonless night.

SOLITARY TREE

Observing Mike slake his thirst through the straw, Sandie again posed her question to him. "Are you my father?"
With a throat that was now hydrated, Mike found that he could at least swallow. Though still feeling the euphoric effects of the drugs, Mike knew that what he said next could alter his whole future. Choosing his words very carefully, Mike decided an attempt at humor might be best. "You're not an angel?" he asked soberly.
Rewarded with the tiniest of smiles, Sandie informed him that she was not an angel.
Attempting to right himself to project a modicum of dignity to their conversation, Mike grimaced with the sudden sharp pulling of the wound.
"Are you alright? Do you need a doctor?" queried Sandie with an anxious look on her face.
"I will be just fine, if you promise not to make me laugh," Mike assured her groggily, managing to paste a sickly-looking smile on his face.
"I believe you asked me a question, and since you have informed me that you're not an angel, though I would be the first to argue that, since you look exactly like an angel I used to know. Are you Sandie Wentworth?" asked Mike quietly.
Unable to speak, Sandie simply nodded her head in the assent.
Slowly extending his large hand Mike introduced himself, and informed Sandie that she was indeed, his long-lost daughter.
Tentatively reaching out to shake the proffered hand, Sandie asked Mike if he had been at the Kal Lake resort.
"Yes," answered Mike. "We had been there for a short vacation, Yolanda, who's your step-mom, talked to you first, when she told me that she was sure it was you I re-entered the office and talked to you."
"Thank-you!" Sandie blurted.
"For what?" asked Mike.
"For saving my sister," she replied wiping a small tear from her cheek.

SOLITARY TREE

Exhausted from this brief conversation with his youngest daughter, Mike told her she was welcome, and unable to deny his body the need for sleep any longer, fell into a deep, healing slumber.

The tumultuous reunion that was a decade in the making, happened on a warm sunny August morning, three weeks after the successful transplant surgery. Both donor and recipient were well on the road to recovery, Mike was experiencing only a rare twinge of discomfort from his suture line, Jasmine with the incredible resilience that youth provides, was enjoying a speedy recovery.

Mike and Yolanda arrived at the Wentworth residence on Kal Lake at eleven in the morning, on what would prove to be a momentous day. When Barry informed Mike that the girls were waiting for him on the dock, Yolanda pressed her lips gently to Mike's cheek and murmured softly that she would wait here with Barry and Jackie while he met his daughters.

 Walking the final sixty steps that separated him and his daughters, Mike was engulfed by a Tsunami of euphoria, which released him from a decade of uncertainty. Stopping four feet away from his two incredibly beautiful daughters, Mike was unable to control the tears of joy that spilled uninterrupted from his eyes.

"I wish to thank-you for donating your kidney to me," initiated Jasmine shyly, as she observed this large man who was her father. That simple statement unleashed a torrent of tears for all parties, as they hugged, cried, and conversed for three heart wrenching hours.

 Wiping her tears Jasmine asked Mike. "What do we call you?"

 Wiping away his own tears Mike replied. "You girls call me whatever you're comfortable with, I would be lying if I said I didn't want to hear you call me dad.

SOLITARY TREE

But, given the circumstances that might be a little awkward, what you girls decide to call me is immaterial, all I have ever wanted I have sitting right in front of me."

One of the more poignant moments in a poignant filled, three-hour conversation, came when Sandie asked about their mother.

Knowing that he had every right to inform the girls that their mother had told Mike. "She was not about to waste her life looking for something that would never be found," instead he gently informed the girls that shortly after the girls had been taken, their mom had left. He informed Jas and Sandie that he and their mother had divorced, and though he had attempted to contact her and apprise her of the fact their girls had been located, he has no idea where she now resides.

Ecstatic at how this reunion was proceeding, Mike was surprised to learn that he had talked to Sandie in the hospital.

She admitted that Mike was loopy at the time, but she stated that she needed to know if he was their Father, just in case something bad happened. Sandie also apprised Mike of the fact that when you're adopted, you never know if you resemble your Father or Mother. "Well we now know who we look like," she declared winking at Mike.

Jasmine then asked the question that Mike had thought would have been asked at the outset of the reunion. "You're not taking us away with you, are you?"

Gazing at both his girls in wonder, enraptured by how beautiful and intelligent they were, Mike answered Jasmine with an emphatic no. "Jackie and Barry are your parents, they have raised you and instilled in you, everything that I had hoped to. You girls belong here, with them as your parents. What I would like to humbly ask you girls is, would you allow Yolanda and myself to spend time with you? We have already located a home in a place called Penticton, about a three-hour drive from here, as I'm sure you girls already know.

SOLITARY TREE

We realize that there is a ten-year gap that cannot be filled, but now that we have found you, we are loath to simply return home. We are prepared to leave the United States as soon as possible, it is our hope that by living in Penticton you girls won't feel pressured to visit us every day, yet still close enough for us to forge a new relationship with you, and be a part of your lives.
  This announcement was cause for another round of hugs, standing there on the dock, overlooking the shimmering water of Kal Lake, with a daughter under each arm, Mike knew the peace and tranquility he was feeling at that very moment, was all that he had ever asked for from life.

About the Author: Robert Lane has been married to his wife Kim for thirty-four years. They reside in the Okanagan Valley, British Columbia. They have two adult sons, and four adorable grandchildren.

Robert Lane would like to take this moment to humbly thank the people who have taken valuable time from their lives to read his novels. His first novel BLURRED LINE was a decade in the making, after allowing the seeds of his idea to germinate then sprout, he announced to his wife that he was ready to write a book. With the success his first book enjoyed, he soon went to work on the sequel SOLITARY TREE, Robert sincerely hopes that readers have enjoyed the sequel as much as they did BLURRED LINE.

CPSIA information can be obtained
at www.ICGtesting.com
Printed in the USA
LVHW03s1101010818
585592LV00003B/496/P

9 781542 814676